WHISPERS OF CONSPIRACY

WHISPS BOOK THREE

JEN HAEGER

SCARSDALE PUBLISHING

TRADEMARK ACKNOWLEDGEMENTS

NYPD
New York State Police
Richter Aero airfield
Bellevue Hospital
CIA
FBI
SWAT
Department of Homeland Security
Human Rights Watch
Gulfstream V
Organisation of Islamic Cooperation
Muslim World League
Tuskegee experiment
The Bourne Identity
A Gentleman in Moscow by Amor Towles
C-12
C-37
WarCraft
USCIS
Bureau of Counterterrorism
Rikers

UN.org
CNN.com
McDonald's
Play-Doh
Dateline
CDC
Department of Defense
www.forbiddenknowledge.com
Freedom of Information Act

For Scott,
"Your crazy matches my crazy. Big time."

ACKNOWLEDGMENTS

A great author once said, "Writing doesn't happen in a vacuum." It's true. Thank you, Casey and Sharona and the Scarsdale Publishing team for all that you do and put up with. Thank you, friends and family for reading, editing, commenting, supporting, and believing in me. And a special thanks to my husband, without whom, I wouldn't be a writer.

CHAPTER 1

Journal Excerpt Dr. Ahmed Mahadow
Wednesday, July 4th, 2029
Full Blast Signal Test: 3:00 a.m. Rubezikan Standard Time
Though previous small-scale tests were positive, preliminary full test results are disastrous. First reports indicate a 25-30% WHISP conversion rate....

L INCOLN IS GONE. M Y BABY IS GONE. A ND IT'S ALL MY fault.

"Sylvy?"

From the concern in Ben's eyes, he's said my name more than once.

"Yeah."

"We're here."

I'd been staring out the window but seeing nothing. Now, the entrance to the precinct looms over us. Before, the sight would've filled my heart with a sense of home, but now, the place is cold, foreign.

Ben clears his throat. "Do you want me to come with you?"

I shake my head. "They'll need you back at the lab. To go over anything...left behind." I open the car door, but he grabs my other hand.

"We'll *find* him."

I nod because I can't speak, not because I believe it.

He squeezes my hand before releasing it. I want to squeeze back, but my hand is numb, my body is numb. I can't feel the pavement beneath my feet as I get out and close the door behind me. A gust of wind catches my coat, throwing it open, but the bitter wind doesn't touch me. The cold comes from within, veins of ice pumping through my frozen heart, every breath a brittle pain in my chest.

I blink and I'm inside the building, crossing the first floor toward the stairs. Someone grabs my arm and spins me around.

"Harbinger!" Crone's face is an unhealthy shade of beetroot. "What are you doing here?"

I throw off his grip, my recently contused elbow screaming in protest. "My job." I turn back toward the stairs but he blocks me.

"No, not like this, you're not. Not right now. Look at yourself. You can barely stand."

"Get out of my way, Crone."

"No."

My fingers flit over the handle of my gun. "Get out of my way."

Crone doesn't budge. "I'm telling you this as your friend. You need to rest. You need to take some time."

"I need to find Lincoln."

"You will, but you won't do it today. Not like this."

"I'll do it any damn way I can and you're wasting time. This isn't your case. Get out of my way."

His eyes meet mine and he steps aside. "I just don't want you to ruin yourself."

I don't reply. His words echo like my footsteps in the stairwell. He doesn't have kids, he can't understand. Whatever happens to me doesn't matter. All I care about is Lincoln.

When I reach the basement, the Task Force floor is buzzing. People are everywhere. *Why wasn't there a response like this to the first kidnapping?* Then I see the state troopers mixed in among the crowd. The first kidnapping was one death and four missing. This is seven deaths and one kidnapping. This is bomb-wired rooms and computers erasing themselves, and evidence and people made to disappear.

"Harbinger?" Green stops in front of me.

"Where are we at?"

Her mouth works a moment before words come out. "Canvasing for witnesses to the Staties' van hit. Problem is, the van was in the middle of nowhere when it happened."

"Have we notified the airports, the border?"

She nods. "We've given them"—she swallows—"Lincoln's description and the best descriptions we have of the prisoners, the situation."

"What about the bodies? Where are we with IDs?"

"Running fingerprints, but no hits yet." Green pauses, winces.

"What?"

"You, um, you're shivering."

I wondered why it was hard to move my mouth properly. "I'll grab some coffee. Warm up." As if that were possible. "Forensics still sweeping the facility?"

She nods. "They aren't very optimistic. These people are too good."

No, no, no. I shake my head. "There has to be something. Nobody's that good."

"Harbinger?"

"Yeah."

"They could've killed him."

My blood turns instantly from ice to magma. "What?"

Green blanches. "I mean, Lincoln's still alive. There's hope."

The magma turns to stone. "I know."

"Okay. Good. Um, get your coffee and, um, there's a briefing in about an hour."

I nod then head to the break area, but when I bend to pick up a cup, my laptop bag strap slides down my arm and I realize I'm still wearing my coat. I weave between bodies and make it to my desk to find it occupied by a Statie. I stand there for a minute but he doesn't look up. I clear my throat.

"I'm kinda busy here." He's flipping through pages from a file.

"My desk."

He finally looks up. "Huh?"

"You're at my desk."

"Oh sorry, there wasn't anyone here." He makes no motions to leave.

My hands clench. Unclench. "I was in the hospital." His badge would just fit into his smug mouth, with a little assistance.

"Glad you're feeling better." He glances around. "There's not much room down here. Any chance we could share?"

Something shifts in the back of my mouth. A tooth. I pry open my jaw, the muscles of the joint creaking in protest. *Get the fuck out of my desk!* I set my laptop down on one side of the desk and take off my coat. I crumple it into a ball and drop it next to the desk. Turning away, I moderate my breathing as I work my way back to the coffee pot. He's working on the case, too, and chewing him out will do nothing productive. The scent of burnt coffee assaults my nose as I pour and my stomach lurches, bile splashing the back of my throat. In spite, I pull out milk from the mini-fridge and dump some into the cup, then add two sugars.

Back at my desk, I retrieve the wadded ball of my coat from

the floor and pull a protein bar from the pocket. Ripping open the bar, I bite half off and chew methodically.

"I think some of the guys are ordering pizza later. You want in?"

I shake my head, the bar's claylike consistency making the mouthful impossible to swallow.

"Suit yourself, but I better not see you bogarting any slices of my meat-lovers."

Finally, the chewed mass goes down my throat. "You seem awfully chipper for just having lost seven of your compatriots." As soon as I speak, I wish I could choke down the words like the protein bar. They're cruel and stupid. A reflection of my own sourness, my own guilt, my own frustration.

The goofy smile melts away, his dark lips stretching thin, veiling his bright white teeth. "Hey, fuck you. I lost friends, good men who didn't deserve to get mowed down over some fucking"—at the last moment, his eyes find Liv and he stumbles in his rant—"research project."

Of course, I don't know exactly what he was about to say, but his face speaks volumes; he is no lover of WHISPs. A spark of anger flares then extinguishes. Who am I to judge? *I'm sorry.* I don't say the words. They'll sound hollow and be a waste of time, of breath. Instead, I shake my head. It doesn't matter. This doesn't matter. Only Lincoln matters. I open my laptop and bring it to life, ignoring my queasiness and the Statie's glare.

I'm not sure what I'm going to work on, what won't be repeating what others are already researching, but I need to do something, anything that feels like progress toward finding Lincoln. Maybe I can find construction permits or, at least, equipment rentals for the farmhouse. Someone had to build that laboratory underneath the barn. I wonder if I can request satellite photos of the area from Google or the NSA or somebody, maybe catch a license plate number or a face entering or leaving the lab. Or maybe I'm getting too fancy, and we should just check security cameras from the local gas stations. People working at the lab couldn't have just ghosted in and ghosted out. *Where to start?* My brain is spinning, but my fingers are idle on the laptop's keyboard. Maybe I should talk to Green first.

"Hey, Keshawn!" A keen, thin Statie is suddenly at my side.

The Statie commandeering half my desk, Keshawn, by his response, looks up. "Yeah, Mattie?"

"My source at that private airstrip came through." He thrusts a printed sheet at Keshawn. "A private jet left the airfield last night headed for Rubezikan. He said he didn't get a good look at who got on the plane but said there were a bunch of trucks and that his boss got paid a stack of bills to keep the flight out of the records and to keep his mouth shut."

"Good work, Mattie, get—"

"Rubezikan?"

Mattie barely spares me a glance. "It's a country in—"

"I know where it is." It's a large, recently and violently formed dictatorship right smack dab in the middle of unethical WHISP research territory. Rubezikan's been all over the news in the few years since its army gouged a new country out of parts of Turkmenistan, Uzbekistan, Tajikistan, and Afghanistan. I snatch the paper from Keshawn's fingers. It looks like a flight plan.

"What the f—"

"They have my son."

I grab my coat off the floor and fish out my phone. The screen complains of a number of missed calls, but I dismiss them all and take a picture of the paper before handing it back to an open-mouthed Keshawn. Standing, I address the other Statie. "Mattie is it?"

"Officer Matheson."

"Fine. Where is this airfield?"

Keshawn stands and raises both hands palms out. "Whoa!

What do you think you're doing? We'll report this at the briefing and State will figure out the best approach. This case may have started in the city, but it's in our jurisdiction now, and I'm not going to have you fuck it up. I'm sorry about your son, really, but I'm not even sure you should be working on this case anymore."

How dare you? Red spots blur my vision, but I take a deep, calming breath. Playing the grief-crazed mother won't earn me any points here. "First, I think you will find that the WHISP Task Force has statewide jurisdiction." *Truth.* "Second, with the chief dead, I'm now in charge of the task force, so I can say who's on it and who isn't." *Possibly true.* I let out the rest of my breath because the truth of my next sentence crushes my heart. "And third, if that plane was carrying my son and really did leave the country, then this case is no longer under either of our jurisdictions anymore."

CHAPTER 2

CIA Communication: Protocol: Whiskey-Sierra-Papa
Status Update: RE: RUBEZIKAN ANOMALY
WHISP anomaly trace COMPLETE
source experimental population calming blast signal
Please advise

THE BRIEFING IS IN JUST A FEW MINUTES, AND Keshawn has finally vacated my desk to go wait in the conference room, giving me a precious few minutes alone to make this phone call. "Jeffrey, I need your help."

"Sylvy? God, I heard what happened. Anything I can do, I'm here. Did they take…Lincoln across state lines?"

I will my voice not to crack. "We think they took him to Rubezikan."

"What?"

"Do you have any contacts in the CIA?"

"Sylvy, I—"

"Christ, Jeffrey, do you?" *Deep breath.* "Do you?"

A heavy sigh. "Even if I did, where would that get you?"

Why does he even have to ask? "Rubezikan."

"That's not the way these things work, and you know that."

"Just get me in touch, Jeffrey. The task force has federal funding. They may see that we can work together on this."

"Sylvy, we need to talk about this. I just—"

Across the room, Green is motioning to me and pointing to the stairs.

"Listen, I've got to go. Just get me an email address or a phone number. Anything. Please." I hang up before he can say something rational and horrible, then join Green at the base of the stairs.

She nods at me and starts up. In my hand, my cell vibrates and I put it on airplane mode as I follow her. When we reach the first floor, Crone is loitering by the conference room door looking sheepish. The look doesn't suit him. I change my mind about ignoring him and wave Green into the room ahead of me.

"What?"

"I'm sorry about before. What I meant to say was, 'This is totally fucked up, what do you need?'"

For the first time since leaving the hospital this morning, tears prick my eyes. "You're not on the task force. But there is an opening." Humor of the darkest shade. I don't even know when the chief's funeral will be. I wonder if Claire had to perform his autopsy.

"I'll talk to Chief Li about a temporary placement, but just until things settle down and you can hire someone else."

Warmth spreads through my chest. I don't have the heart to tell him the truth, that they've probably taken Lincoln out of the country and there's only the slimmest hope the task force will be able to follow the case overseas. "Don't you have your own cases?"

He shrugs. "Nothing Thompson or Hardcastle can't handle."

"Well, then you'd better come in."

Inside, although all the chairs are occupied, the conference room isn't quite full, yet it feels claustrophobic. Flashes of my brief quarantine here bombard my sanity, but I push the memories away. They will only lead me down the path to where I involved my son in a case that put his life in danger.

At the front of the room, standing behind a podium, is a man I don't recognize, staring the gathered crowd into silence. Once the chatter dies down, he clears his throat. "For those of you who don't know me, I'm Carter Jackson, Superintendent of the New York State Police force. What happened two nights ago was nothing short of an atrocity, but we aren't here to mourn our fellow officers. Not yet. We're here now to work together with the WHISP Task Force to bring justice to the fallen. Here's what we know…"

As he speaks, my throat closes and my ears fill with cotton. I can't hear what happened coming from someone outside it all. Having been there, I relive it every time I close my eyes. Filling the seconds, I breathe in and hold my breath until my chest aches, then let it out. I blink and someone else is at the podium, another Statie. I'd missed her name. She's in charge of the canvas in the area where the State Police van was assaulted, but she doesn't have much to contribute. The area was fairly isolated and none of the people questioned had heard anything unusual or seen anything unusual that night.

"Must've used silencers," Crone mumbles.

Preparation. That wasn't a desperate attempt to rescue their people, it was a planned assault, methodical. But we already knew that. I nod.

Next, Green takes the podium and gives a rundown on the forensic evidence from the farmhouse and laboratory, which is basically nothing but some poorly defined tire tracks and smeared prints. Someone asks her about ballistics.

"We won't have the ballistics back until tomorrow at the earliest."

No, of course not. They had to fish most of the bullets out of dead bodies and they'll need to be cleaned of adhered flesh and blood. I picture Claire delicately removing the bullet from the chief's chest and mine aches. He probably wouldn't have asked to head the WHISP Task Force if it hadn't been for me.

Green returns to her place along the wall and Beaulieu from Cyber stands to take the podium but she doesn't have much to say. They're working with CompUServer Plus again, with some new software, trying to recover data from the lab's hard drives.

Nothing. Nothing. Nothing. How can we still have nothing?

Finally, officer Matheson gets behind the podium. "So, we do have one lead we believe to be pretty solid. A contact of mine at Richter Aero airfield in Essex reported a private jet leaving that airfield with an unknown number of people aboard headed for the country of Rubezikan."

No one had been talking up until now, still, a profound silence blankets the conference room. It's like someone pressed the pause button. Nobody moves. Nobody breathes.

"Did he just say Rubezikan? Fucking Rubezikan?"

Crone. Of course, it would be Crone to break the silence.

I nod. "Yeah."

"Fuck, Harbinger, I... Fuck."

I don't look at him. I can't. "Yeah."

The room doesn't erupt in chatter, but a hiss and murmur rolls through the crowd. Superintendent Jackson displaces Matheson at the podium and raises a hand. The room quiets once more.

"Until we're able to verify this lead"—he glances at Matheson, sizing him up—"*if* we are able to verify it, I expect all of you to continue working as though these bastards are still in New York. We don't know for sure they've gone, but if anyone involved in this is still in New York, still in North America, I expect us to find them." He punches his left hand with his right fist. "Dismissed."

Slowly, early arrivals who snagged seats rise, and the rest of us start shuffling toward the door. Crone turns to me. "You don't really think… I mean, fucking Rubezikan? I'm not even sure I can find that on a fucking map."

"Yeah. I do."

"And…your son. You think they took him?"

Oh please, God, let it not be true. "Yeah. I do."

We're out in the hall now, vaguely angling toward the stairs with the rest of the task force and Staties, but Crone grabs my arm and drags me into an empty observation room adjacent to one of the interrogation rooms. Shutting the door behind us, he turns to me. "What are you going to do?"

I blink at him. "What do you mean?"

He gives me his cut-the-bullshit face. "Harbinger, I know we were only partners for like five minutes or whatever, but give me a little credit. I'm a detective, too. They took your son to fucking Rubezikan. What are you going to do?"

I could lie, but I don't. "I asked my friend in the FBI to get me in contact with someone at the CIA."

He nods, no hint of surprise visible. "You think that'll work?"

"The task force is federally funded, at least partially. I'm hoping that'll give me some kind of leg to stand on with them."

He lets out a long breath. "And if it doesn't?"

As if Crone's opened a valve in my heart and all the air is rushing out, I'm deflating, shrinking. "What else can I do?"

Working his jaw back and forth, he frowns. "I'll get with vice. See what the four-one-one is with the Rubezikan mob. There's gotta be one. All those countries have cancer clusters of crime bosses in New York."

"What are you talking about? How will that help? It's not like I can pass as a Rubezikani woman."

"What? No shit. No, I'm thinking about intel. Vice may

have someone on the inside. Someone who might be able to get over there and get us some more information."

I want to tell him I'm not going to have some poor under-cover slob sliced into little bits for me, but then I remember that it isn't for me, it's for Lincoln. Ice prickles my chest. "Do it."

CIA Communication: Protocol: Whiskey-Sierra-Papa
Response: RE: RUBEZIKAN ANOMALY
Monitor situation await further instruction
copy
known WHISP conversions?
estimate 30%
among operatives?
_1%_

BACK AT MY DESK, NOW BLESSEDLY VACATED, I CHECK my cell for a text from Jeffrey. There are even more missed calls now, and a couple of texts from Ben, but I ignore them, turning to my email. Again, there are several emails from Ben, but none from Jeffrey. *Dammit! Come on!*

I stand and grab my coat, intending to demand Matheson take me to the airfield when Ben comes bounding down the stairs. *Shit.* I throw my coat back down and watch him walk over instead of going to him.

"What are you doing here?" I can't keep the impatience out of my voice.

Hurt cuts through the concern on his face and is replaced by a weary anger. "You're not answering your phone, or your emails, what am I supposed to do?"

"We were in a briefing."

He opens his mouth, shakes his head, closes it, then starts again. "Sylvy, the hospital called. They said they got some test results back and need to speak to you."

Irrelevant. I sink into my seat and pinch my forehead as needles of pain stab my frontal lobe. "I'll call them tomorrow."

Ben stares me down. "No, you won't."

He's right. "I'm sure it's nothing. Probably just checking on my miraculously not broken arm." A brittle laugh dies in my throat. My son is being experimented on by bioterrorists in Rubezikan and my doctor wants to discuss how often I'm icing my elbow.

"Maybe, and if it is you can tell them to fuck off, but will you *please* call them?"

It's Ben's use of the f-word that makes me look up. He swears much less than I do. It's then I see the terror in the creases of his face. He's already lost a son. He's worried about losing his wife, too. I glance at the clock: 4:22 p.m. Unfortunately, there's still time to call back the doctor today. My fingers twitch toward the landline phone, but before I reach for it, Ben asks, "Is there any news about…about Lincoln?"

A flood. The other reason he's here in person, besides the doctor's message. He thinks I'm hiding things from him, thinks I know something bad. I do. *Oh God, Ben.* How can I tell him our son is in Rubezikan? He might as well be on the moon. He might as well be… No, I can't even think that. I can't meet his eye.

"There's one lead we're looking into right now." My voice cracks, and I refresh my e-mail in-box so I can glance away. Ben doesn't let the silence stretch.

"And? What is it?"

Still no email from Jeffrey. Instead of Ben, I address the

computer screen. "There was a flight out of an airfield in upstate New York. A private jet headed overseas. We think it had the escapees from the lab raid onboard."

Ben's hand is on my shoulder, squeezing. "And Lincoln?"

I nod.

"Overseas?"

I nod. His hand is a vice. The fingers of my right arm tingle from blood loss.

"Overseas where, Sylvy?"

I breathe in deeply through my nose, the air tainted by sweat, stale coffee, pizza, and a faint waft of basement mildew. "Rubezikan."

Suddenly, all the life leaves Ben's hand and blood rushes back into my arm in a painful wave of warmth. His voice is dry and empty. "Rubezikan?"

I nod. I have to look at him now. It would be too cruel to leave him alone in his own world of desperation. He wobbles and I stand to grip him in a hopeless embrace.

He breathes into my ear. "Rubezikan? But that's where..."

Where all of the worst news about brutal WHISPer human rights violations are coming from. I hug him tighter. "I know."

Ben pulls away. "What can we do?"

There's no sense telling Ben about the CIA or vice if nothing comes of either. It'll just upset him. "I'm working on it. The first step is to verify as best we can that the private jet is involved. Right now, we only have an informant's word. We need to shake down the flight controller there, see if we can trace the aircraft on other airport radar, maybe military radar, and exhaust all other leads. Then we can appeal to maybe the State Department?" I'm just talking now. Words as balm, even if they have no meaning.

"Are you going to the airfield?"

I shake my head. "The Staties are handling it."

Suspicion, like a shadow, falls over Ben's face.

Backpedal, Sylvy. "I was dead set on going, but since the chief's gone, I'm kinda acting head of the task force right now, so I have to stay here and coordinate."

Ben's mouth opens, but the phone on my desk chooses this moment to jangle to life. Glad for the distraction, I snatch up the receiver. "Harbinger."

"Detective, I have a Doctor Sanchez from Bellevue Hospital on the line for you. She says it's urgent. Would you like me to put her through?"

Ben is bracing for bad news. I shake my head slightly and mouth the word "hospital." "Sure, put her through." I guess this saves me the trouble of calling the hospital or coming up with an excuse to not call. There's a click and a hiss as the call is transferred through the ancient precinct switchboard.

"Detective Harbinger?" the voice is youngish and feminine, but gruff from exhaustion and irritation.

"Yes, speaking."

"Sylvia Harbinger?"

Get on with it. My eyes find the ceiling. "Yes."

"We've been trying to reach you all day."

"Yes, I know, I'm sorry. I've..." *Do I really want to get into why I've been ignoring the calls?* "I'm sorry."

A heavy sigh. "I need to give you some test results. Are you sitting down?"

Am I sitting down? Without warning, all the "connection" I've felt between Liv and me resolves into a much simpler explanation: brain tumor. *But they wouldn't give me results like those over the phone, would they?*

"Detective?"

"Yes, I'm sitting down."

"You're pregnant," she lilts the second word.

Certain I've misheard, I can barely force sound from my throat. "What?"

My face is hiding nothing, and Ben drops to his knees next

to me. His face is bleached-flour white, but his lips are red. "What is it, Sylvy?"

"I said, you're pregnant, Detective. It's a standard test we run whenever a patient has passed out. Have you noticed any dizziness, nausea, or heartburn lately?"

Unquestionably, it's only in my head, but even so, Liv's tinkling laughter echoes around me.

Ben grabs my wrist. "Sylvy?"

I shake my head. There must be some mistake. "I'm fifty-four."

A chuckle. "Yes, well, that's why we'd like you to come back to the hospital for some additional tests. Later life pregnancies have additional health risks, and"—Dr. Sanchez clears her throat—"you may want to speak to a counselor about your...options."

Options? What the hell? "Options?"

A soft cough. "Yes. Some women your age choose not to proceed with the pregnancy due to the adverse risks to their own health. We can set up an appointment to run certain tests and then when the results come back, I can sit down with you and talk about the risks in your case, and then, if you're still uncertain, we can set up an appointment with a hospital counselor."

Tests? Appointments? My son is in Rubezikan! I don't have time for this. "I'm.... I'll have to call you back."

"Well, I'd like to schedule those tests now if—"

Placing the receiver back on the cradle, I can't help noticing cracks in the institution-yellow cord. *How many years does this antique have left in it? Will they replace it with a cordless phone or another antique with a curling, springy, baby-puke colored cord?*

"Sylvy?"

The agony on Ben's face brings me back. "I'm pregnant."

His face collapses in on itself in confusion. "What?"

"That's what I said."

CHAPTER 4

Encrypted Communication: President Alperen Pargulmahamadomet
Dear Most Honorable President Pargulmahamadomet:
The CIA has become aware of the unfortunate circumstances regarding the recent WHISP outbreak in your
country. We, ourselves, have been working on the
WHISP dilemma and would like to extend aid in mitiga-
tion/elimination efforts in exchange for access to
subjects suitable for WHISP research. We await your
response.
With great respect,
Martin Exavier Ruftin, CIA Executive Director of WHISP
Affairs

BEN'S GAZE FINDS MY STOMACH THEN MY EYES AGAIN.
"Pregnant?"

My hand goes to my belly as if I could feel anything this
early. Now it all makes crazy sense. This is what Liv wasn't
telling me. This is why my readings were screwed up, not

because of some virus. I can almost hear her in my head, or maybe I do. *You knew this.* I nod.

Ben's mouth is working but no sound is coming out.

One of us has to keep it together. "They want me to go into the hospital for additional tests and to discuss options."

The two furry beasts of his eyebrows knit. "Options?"

Damn. I shouldn't have said anything about options. "On birthing plans." Not a total lie. One plan would be to not go ahead with the birth. *Is that a plan? What is the plan? Shit.* There's almost no chance I'm going to be able to get in with the CIA and get to Rubezikan, but there's zero chance they're going to send in a pregnant woman. It would make everything so much easier if it all just went away. At this point, it would be an outpatient procedure. I'd be back on my feet within eight to twelve hours.

My hand is still on my stomach.

Ben places his hand over mine, a whisper of a smile on his face. "Guess we've been a little reckless."

With his words, the last few months flood my thoughts. As much as I've been struggling with Liv, in retrospect, those months were a blissful dream: new jobs, crashing with Lincoln like college kids. *Lincoln.* My heart squeezes as warmth and nausea wash over me. *Had I really forgotten about him, even for a second?* He's the most important thing right now. This can wait. If I do nothing, no one will even know. I take Ben's hand in both of mine, then glance around the room. Everyone's still bustling around or taking a quiet breather. Nobody's looking at us. "It's good we know what the hospital wanted to talk to me about, but we have to focus on Lincoln right now."

Ben opens his mouth, but I squeeze his hand.

"This is not an emergency. This can wait."

Closing his mouth, he nods solemnly then glances around the room, stands, and wipes tears from the corners of his eyes. "Are you coming home tonight?"

Something to consider, as it might be the last chance I have, and I may need my passport. I push away thoughts of how empty and hollow the apartment feels without Lincoln. "Yeah, but I need to finish up a few things here before I go, double check that I'm in the loop on all of our leads, make sure the Staties aren't keeping anything to themselves."

He points to the chair I pulled up earlier. "Can I wait here?"

"Sure."

———

IN THE BLINK OF AN EYE, WE'RE HOME, OR, AT LEAST, back at Lincoln's apartment wishing it still felt like a home. I struggle to remember what I said to Green before we left. Did I talk to anyone else? Yes, the Statie Superintendent. Jackson? What did I say to him? Something about being the temporary head of the WHISP Task Force now that the chief.... Does it matter?

"Are you hungry?"

I shake my head, but my belly protests loud enough for Ben to hear.

He nods and kisses my forehead. "I'll make us some eggs."

I follow him partway down the hall, but turn into the guest bedroom, our bedroom, instead. This is where it happened. I shrug off the thought. *Lincoln.* The weight of my sorrow makes the bed groan as I drop onto it. Nothing is more tempting than sinking down and pulling the covers over my head until my tears soak the sheets, but I can't fall apart now, can't let Lincoln down. I pull out my phone and check again for a reply from Jeffrey. There's an email from an unfamiliar address with the subject heading "Ludo Casilla" and a phone number. My heart stops mid-beat and restarts painfully as I suck in a breath. This is it. Jeffrey came through. Really, it's nothing. The odds of this Casilla working with me through the thin veil of the task force is nearly nil, but I have to draw some hope.

Ben sticks his head in and I close the screen, turning the phone face down against the comforter.

If he notices my guilty motions or the flush in my cheeks or the lump in my throat, he shows no sign. "Eggs are ready."

I nod, force a grim smile. "I'll be there in a minute."

He retreats. The hand gripping my cell screams in agony. With effort, I release the phone and kneel next to the bed. Groping underneath it, my hand encounters first a disgruntled Grumps the Cat, then a small suitcase. With heart racing, I dig through the outer pockets. My passport is in the second one. I stash it in my computer bag then shove the suitcase back under the bed and stand. I won't be able to smuggle out a suit-case or even a duffle bag without Ben noticing. *Do I still have a change of clothes in my locker at the station?* I think so. One thing at a time. I pocket my cell and head into the kitchen to pretend to eat.

"HOW DID YOU GET THIS NUMBER?"

Not sure what I was expecting, but the gravelly anger on the other end of the line makes my throat tighten. To be fair, it is two in the morning, but I couldn't wait any longer, and it took Ben longer to fall asleep than usual. "Jeffery Kearn with the FBI."

An irritable sigh and colorful, under-breath curse. "You have one minute. Go."

"My name is Sylvia Harbinger. I'm the acting head of the New York City WHISP Task Force."

"So what?"

My opportunity to help Lincoln is slipping through my fingers. I scramble for something to hook agent Casilla. "So, a plane full of WHISP bioterrorists left an airfield in upstate New York two days ago, headed for Rubezikan."

"And?"

"And I want in." I catch myself too late. "The task force wants in."

"In on what?"

My molars ache from clenching my jaw. "On the pursuit, on the mission."

The minute must be up now, so I breathe again when he answers, "What makes you think there'll be any action?"

"They're bioterrorists who perpetrated crimes in the United States, and—" my voice catches in my throat.

"And?"

I swallow three times in quick succession. "And they have a hostage. An American citizen."

Another sigh, less angry than the first. "Your son."

My mouth gapes open. "How..."

"Of course, we know what's going on. We've been monitoring the situation since we became aware of anti-WHISP terrorist activity in New York City."

White hot rage floods my body. "And you did nothing?" *Shit.* My voice is too loud. I glance toward the hallway, to the bedroom door.

"Not our thing."

"But it is now, and I want in." My words scrape my throat raw.

"The task force, you mean."

"Right."

"Don't call this number again."

"Wait!"

The line clicks dead. As tears well, my fingers fumble to redial. Halfway through the number, my hands are shaking so badly I drop the phone. *I've blown it.* I let the phone lay on the couch cushion and, instead, bring my hands to my mouth to muffle my sobs. *Shhhh. Shhhh. This isn't over.* I just need another contact. Maybe a congressman? My phone buzzes softly. I flip it over and find a text from a blocked number.

Unknown: 1700 21st Street Suite B, noon.

Hope, like a bird, explodes in my chest. Heart galloping, I swallow back my disappointment. *I'm coming, Lincoln. Hang on. I'm coming.*

CHAPTER 5

Encrypted Communication President Alperen Pargulma-
hamadomet: CIA
Executive Director:
The great country of Rubezikan declines the assistance
of foreign spies and murderers. Whatever WHISP
rumors about our country you have heard are false.
With all respect due to you and the country you repre-
sent, Go Fuck Yourself,
Highest and Most Honorable, Venerable, and
Worshipped President Alperen Pargulmahamadomet

I PARK THREE BLOCKS AWAY FROM THE ADDRESS
Casilla texted, don my going-to-meet-a-CIA-operative
sunglasses, and head down the street, passport in my pocket,
but leave my duffel with extra clothes on the passenger's seat. I
don't want to seem presumptuous. The fact that he's set a
meeting is a good sign, but the CIA working with the task force
is one thing, them taking me with them to Rubezikan is
another.

It's another cold, clear day, but the sunlight is chilled and too bright for me as I scan up and down the street. There's a couple walking a dog ahead on the other side, but I'm distracted by the trio of suited men walking toward me—could they be agents?—but they pass without a glance in my direction. Then a bicycle courier shoots past me, and I nearly pull my gun. *Easy, Harbinger. Keep it together. How are you going to function in a foreign country if you can't even walk down a street in your own state?*

After what feels more like twelve blocks than three, I reach a nondescript office building with a revolving door. Being slightly claustrophobic, I choose one of the normal doors to the side, but find it locked. Sighing, I push through the revolving door as quickly as possible and find myself in a very plain atrium last decorated sometime in the 1970s. A plaque on the wall informs me that Suite B is on the second floor, and another sign points me toward the elevators. No stairs are evident, so I follow the arrows around a corner to the bank of elevators and press the call button.

As I wait, the stillness of the building presses in on me. Nothing is stirring. I can't even discern the clank and hiss of a boiler. The air is warmer than outside though, so the heat must be running. Also, under the stringent scent of cleaner is the distinct aroma of old dust. When the elevator dings, it's way too loud and sends my heart racing for the exit. When the door opens, I half expect an armed assassin, but it's empty and banal. *I watch way too many spy movies.* I enter and press the metal button next to the slightly crooked 2. The building has six floors. I wonder if any of the others are occupied or if the rest of the building is just a façade.

The elevator bings again and I straighten before the doors open. Ahead is an empty hallway with a dingy linoleum floor, off white walls, and a drop ceiling accented with cheap, fluorescent lights. The windows at either end of the hallway let in streaky daylight and highlight colonies of dust motes. When I step out, I'm sure that I'm the only human being in the building, yet am still being watched. I scan for cameras, but if there are any, they're well-hidden. The door has Suite B stenciled on it in neat letters. Reaching for the handle, I pause and hold my breath, listening. Nothing. Is this whole thing some kind of test or is this just how the CIA operates? *Way too many spy movies.* I grab the handle.

Even though the door isn't heavy enough to be soundproofed, when I open it, a flood of noise drifts out: The tick-tapping of a man seated before a computer at a desk that faces the door, the distant chime of an office phone, its insistent ringing ignored, and the aquatic burble of a fish tank in the corner of what could be mistaken for a dentist's reception area. I approach the desk, but the man doesn't look up or stop typing.

"I'm here to see—"

"Third door on the right, Detective."

It's then I notice a subtle wireless earpiece, much fancier than the ones SWAT uses, tucked into his ear.

"Um, thanks." Smooth.

I pass the desk, find the third unmarked door, and wonder briefly if I should knock before walking in. It's probable Casilla will respect and appreciate directness more than politeness, so I open the door and head in. His office is, well, probably not, in fact, his office. The shelves are empty, the walls and windows are bare, and the desk, chairs, and file cabinet look like office surplus. Casilla glances up from a very shiny laptop, checks his watch, and nods with grim satisfaction.

"Right on time. Sit." He snaps the laptop closed and motions to the seats in front of the desk. "So, what can the WHISP Task Force offer us?"

I've anticipated this question, but my answer still sounds a bit anemic as I take the seat closest to the small window. "To start, we can offer access to the terrorists' underground laboratory in Upstate New York, access to the victims who were experimented on there, and access to our research and findings regarding the WHISP virus they developed."

Casilla is understandably unimpressed. "All right. Assuming the agency doesn't already have access to those things or the authority to force you to give us access, what do you want in return?"

"Eyes on the ground in Rubezikan."

He stares me down. "You mean, you on the ground in Rubezikan."

"I…." I'm struggling for a bullshit reason it needs to be me but haven't managed to come up with one yet. "Yes."

"Impossible."

"Why?"

One eyebrow hitches up. "You do realize that Rubezikan is one of the most dangerous anti-WHISP countries in the world—"

Lincoln. My heart catches in my chest. "Yes."

"—and that you have a WHISP."

Fuck you, Liv. Scrambling now, "You could use me as bait."

Casilla leans back in his chair and sighs. "Not going to happen. You're too emotionally involved. He's your son, for Christ sakes. You wouldn't let a grieving mother help you with a mur—with one of your investigations. Why should we?"

"Because I'm a cop, and a detective, and the head of the WHISP Task Force, and a mother."

He shakes his head, but I pull out my ace in the hole.

"And because I'm the only one who can cure the virus."

His eyes narrow. "You mean, you're the only one who knows how to cure the virus."

"No, I'm the only one who *can* cure it. Who *has* cured it."

"How exactly?"

"I used L—my WHISP."

Casilla is sitting up straighter now. "You used your WHISP to cure a WHISP virus. How does that work?"

Bingo. "I'm not sure I can explain it."

"Can't or won't?"

A little of both. "Does that mean I'm in?"

His jaw works like he's chewing on his next words. "Are you really willing to put yourself out there as bait for a WHISP terrorist organization?"

"To save my son? Absolutely."

What about her?

I will my hand not to go to my belly. *Shut up, Liv.*

Casilla opens his mouth, but there's a knock at the door. Instead of speaking, he motions me to take cover with a gun that's materialized in his hand. Ducking beside the door, I pull my gun and prepare to cover him.

He levels his gun at the door. "Yes?"

"Sir. She was followed."

Casilla lowers the gun and sighs before shooting me a *give-me-a-break* look. This does not look good for me. *Who could be following me?* I wrack my brain. Not the terrorists. As far as we could tell, they'd all fled the country, and I didn't really have anything they wanted…not anymore. Not unless they'd found out I'd cured the kidnapping victims. *But how could they?* Maybe Crone checking up on me? I had gone AWOL before under his nose when I got thrown off the Chester copycat case. He might be trying to make sure I didn't do something stupid again. Touching, but if he ruins this for me, I'll never forgive him.

Casilla flips open his laptop, examines the screen, then turns it around to face me. "Recognize your tail?"

I holster my gun and approach the desk. The computer screen is divided into quarters, each showing a video feed. One is of the second-floor hallway, one is of the inside of the elevator, one is the empty lobby, and the last is a wide angle of the front of the building showing a man sitting in a car. *Shit.*

"Well?"

I nod. "Yeah."

"Who is it?"

I drop into one of the chairs and put my head in my hands. "My husband."

CHAPTER 6

Encrypted Communication: President Alperen Pargulma-
hamadomet
President Alperen Pargulmahamadomet:
The CIA would like to remind you of certain terms
agreed to in the repression of the 2019 coup by General
Shohrat Niyazova. In other words, You Owe Us. We
would hate to hear of another similar, but successful
coup. Non-negotiable terms of your cooperation in this
matter are attached.
Awaiting your prompt response,
Martin Exavier Ruftin, CIA Executive Director of WHISP
Affairs

"YOU'VE GOT TO BE JOKING," CASILLA SAYS.

I look up at him. "I wish I was."

"You didn't realize your own husband was following you?"

"He didn't follow me, I'm sure of it." I shake my head. "He probably went through the messages on my cell phone when I was in the shower this morning."

"And I take it you didn't delete my message?" Casilla shakes his head in disgust.

I stare him down. "So, I'm new to the spy business, sue me."

"This is exactly what I'm talking about."

"I wouldn't let anyone else get that close to me."

Casilla spins his laptop back around. "Not even your son?"

My son? "What?"

"They could use him to get to you. To get to us."

"I wouldn't let that happen."

Casilla rolls his eyes. "You wouldn't even know it was happening."

The opportunity is slipping through my fingers like sand. *Ben, what have you done? No, Sylvy, don't you fucking give up.* "He could be an asset."

"Who? Hubby dearest? That's just what we need."

"If you did your homework, you know he's on the task force, too. He's head of the WHISP particle research lab."

"And how exactly would he be an asset in Rubezikan?"

The wheels in my brain are spinning. "He's a scientist. Given the right...credentials, he could pass for an anti-WHISP researcher fleeing the States."

"And you think these terrorists would accept him into the fold with open arms?"

Depends on if CAW and Lila Grant have actually turned over a new leaf. "Maybe, if he already had a contact within the group."

"So, you're willing to get yourself and your husband killed to save your son? You sure he feels the same way?"

I nod. "What have you got to lose anyway? Either we help and you take down the bad guys, or we help and fail to take them down, get killed, and no one has a clue we were working with you. You might get an edge on the terrorists regardless of whether my family makes it out alive. Sounds like a win-win situation to me."

Casilla's face is a mask again. "I think you should go down and talk to your husband."

"That's not a no."

"Isn't it?"

———

I SLIP OUT THE BACK DOOR OF THE OFFICE BUILDING and approach Ben's car from behind. No doubt, Casilla is watching, so I want to prove that I can be stealthy enough to sneak up on my own husband. I knock on the passenger's side window and Ben jumps in his seat, spilling coffee in his lap. When he sees me, he winces and unlocks the door. I get in as he dabs his pants with an old fast-food napkin.

"You're following me?" An accusation more than a question. I know his heart's in the right place, so I don't want to hate him for this, but if he's blown my only chance to help Lincoln….

He crushes the damp napkin in his hand and deposits it in the door pocket without looking at me. "You didn't give me much choice, did you? Our son in Rubezikan, you off to some secret meeting, what did you expect me to do?"

"Respect my privacy and not go into my phone when I'm in the shower."

He finally looks at me with haunted eyes. "Sylvy, we've been married a long time. I know you. I knew you were keeping something from me. I've let it slide before because you did it to protect me and Lincoln, but not this time. Lincoln is my son, too, and we're both on the task force. I need you to let me in. I need you to tell me everything. I'm not losing you both."

As if barbed, words catch in my throat. He's right. And if I'm honest, I needed him before to save Lincoln, and I need him again. I nod.

"So, tell me."

"Jeffrey connected me with the CIA. I was in there trying to convince them to work with the task force and let me go with them to Rubezikan."

He nods. "And?"

I glance over at the building and collapse slightly into myself. "It was a long shot before they spotted you. Now...." I shake my head and rub the start of tears from my eyes.

"Could we threaten them with exposure or bad publicity or something if they don't take us?"

"I don't really think.... Wait, us?"

There's steel in Ben's gaze. "You are not going alone."

My defensive, you-can't-tell-me-what-I-can-and-cannot-do hackles bristle.

You need him.

Not now, Liv. Ha, I wouldn't be alone. Not by a long shot. I shake Liv off. "The only real leverage I have is that I'm the only one who's cured the WHISP virus." *I think.* As far as I know, every hostage who made it out of the terrorist lab is still alive.

He taps his fingers on the steering wheel and stares past me. "We may have more. We may have developed the only way of detecting the virus, as well."

"But I never had the virus. Liv said my WHISP readings were off because I'm...." Why is it so hard to say the word right now?

"Pregnant? That might make sense." He nods. "But that doesn't mean our theory wasn't sound. In fact, it may even validate our ability to detect WHISP abnormalities."

"What if each WHISP is just totally different? Totally unique?"

He focuses on me again. "I don't think so. Your and Lincoln's baselines weren't—"

My cell rings. I pull it from my pocket and glance down at the screen: Crone. *Shit.* That's all I need, is two babysitters. I answer, planning on a lame, overslept-my-alarm excuse. "Hey, Crone, sorry I—"

"Harbinger, I don't know where the Hell you are, but you'd better get your ass down to the precinct right now."

My spine stiffens. "Why, what's going on?"

"The feds are back."

CHAPTER 7

Excerpt Personal Diary: Dr. Ahmed Mahadow
Tuesday, July 24th, 2029
Project Arvoh is scheduled to continue as planned in my absence, headed by Dr. Abdullayev. I have many reservations about working with the CIA, but the president is insistent upon our full cooperation. My flight to New York leaves in 12 hours. It seems strange to go there when we have so many experimental subjects here, but I'm assured the facilities in New York are much grander and more advanced than those in Yedys....

"THE FBI? WHO THE HELL CALLED THEM IN?" *JEFFREY?* No. Technically, it's a kidnapping, but since they left the country, Lincoln's abduction shouldn't be in their jurisdiction. Besides, he wouldn't do something like that without telling me.

"Not the FBI."

"What?" I glance back up at the office building.

"Badge I saw was for the Department of Homeland Security, but whatever, they're all goddamn feds. And they're taking over our case. So, are you coming or do Green and I have to try to fend them off all by ourselves?"

My mind is racing. Is this some bullshit power play on Casilla's part to show me just how little leverage I have, or is this a case of your typical government bureaucracy and the right hand not knowing what the left hand is doing? "Okay, okay, I'll be right there." As I stash my phone back in my pocket, I turn to Ben. "Babe, can you drive me to my car? It's a couple of blocks up."

He nods and starts the car. "What's going on?"

"I'm not entirely sure. Either the CIA is trying to put me in my place, or Homeland Security just decided to muscle in on the case."

"Oh. Well, if it is Homeland Security, then isn't that good? Wouldn't that be even more resources going towards find-ing"—he swallows hard—"finding Lincoln?"

"Maybe." I shake my head. "I don't know. It might just be more red tape we need to cut through to get to him, to get him out."

He pulls up next to my car and stops. "Do you think it would help if I was there?"

"No." I open the door. "No, I'll call you when I can and let you know what's going on." I've got one foot out the door when he touches my arm. The bruised elbow twinges with pain.

"Promise?"

A part of me wants to lean back in and kiss him, but I don't. "I promise."

———

BACK AT THE PRECINCT, ALL IS CHAOS. SHOUTS ECHO in the stairwell before I'm halfway down the stairs, and I nearly bowl over a suit carrying a box of files.

"Excuse me," he says.

I don't get out of his way. "I'm sure you have a warrant for those?"

He steps to one side and rolls his eyes. "Take it up with the director."

Resisting the urge to trip him—is it a federal offense to assault a federal agent?—I take the rest of the stairs two at a time, but when I reach the bottom, a wave of nausea makes me pause. *Why couldn't it be another boy?*

Musical laughter.

I was never sick when I was pregnant with Lincoln. My heart seizes for a split second and I take a deep breath to restart it. *Lincoln.* I scan the room for a suit that looks more arrogant than the rest, but Crone spots me first and trundles over.

"Took you long enough."

"Sorry. Who's the man in charge?"

"Woman, actually. Name's Hana Siddiqui. She was pretty pissed you weren't here when she showed up at 9:00 a.m., being the temporary head of the task force and all."

Now that Crone's narrowed my options, Siddiqui stands out. Even in two-inch heels, she's shorter than I'd expect for a director of Homeland Security, but her stature doesn't seem to be an issue as she orders her posse around our department. I straighten my jacket. It's a good thing I dressed up for the CIA this morning. "All right, let's do this." I take a few strides toward Siddiqui, but then notice Crone isn't moving. "Aren't you coming?"

"Nah. I already had the pleasure. I'll watch the show from over here."

I shrug like it doesn't matter, but my stomach tightens as I approach the director alone. Either she doesn't notice me, or she's ignoring me, so I extend my hand. "Ms. Siddiqui? My name's Detective Harb—"

She doesn't take my hand or look up from a folder she's perusing. "I know *who* you are. What I'm more interested to know is if it's standard procedure for the head of a federal task force to come waltzing in around ten in the morning. I'm sure the State Department will be glad to know their money is being wasted on people who can't even bother to show up."

I want to tell her that normally I don't come in at 7:00 a.m. because either I'm still here from the day before or I've only just gotten home an hour or two before that, but she doesn't care. She's pissed and I'm her whipping boy. The real point is, she expected me to be here, which probably means she's not working with Casilla. At this point, I have no idea if that's a good thing or a bad thing. "I had a personal matter to take care of this morning. If I'd've known you were coming, I would've changed my appointment and brought in donuts. But I'm here now, so why don't you tell me what's going on?"

Siddiqui snaps the folder closed and finally meets my eye. "What's going on is that, as of an hour ago, Homeland Security is now in charge of this possible terrorist attack, and you need to make sure that we get all of your records regarding this case by the end of the day."

"Of course. I'll personally make sure that everyone here makes the case transition as smooth as possible and provides your staff with their full cooperation. I'll just first need to make sure all the I's are dotted and T's crossed on that federal court order."

She clears her throat. "It's coming."

The Hell? "I'm sorry?"

"The court order."

"The court order what?"

Straightening her shoulders and lifting her chin, Siddiqui gains about half an inch. "Is coming."

I still have about an inch on her, and I use every bit of it, not bothering to moderate my voice in any way. "You don't have a court order?"

A few of the closest members of the task force stop dead and stare.

"It'll be here any minute. I was just being efficient." Her eyelid just barely twitches.

Maybe she is working with Casilla and planned on me not being here. "Efficient? We have a different term for doing something illegal around here."

"I was just following—"

"Since you weren't following procedure, you probably don't want to finish that sentence. In fact, what you're going to want to do is tell your people to stop what they're doing, bring all our files back to the department, sit on their hands, and wait for the court order to come through."

"Detective, you and I both know that it's only a matter of time before that court order comes through. Why make this harder for everyone? Especially yourself. After all, we're all on the same team here. I would think you'd want us to use every resource possible to get your son back."

Oh no. You do not get to talk about my son.

I turn to Green, who just happens to be one of the people in earshot of our conversation. "Detective Green, it turns out the Department of Homeland Security doesn't have a court order to take over this case. Can you please see that their people immediately stop what they're doing and return any files they've already taken?"

Green's smile is predatory. "Be happy to, Chief."

I know why she used the word in front of Siddiqui, because it sounds much more official than "temporary task force head," but it's not right and it triggers a stab of pain in my heart. I direct that pain right at Siddiqui. "There is no *we* in this process. Your department wasn't coming in to offer its resources to the task force in some joint effort. You were sneaking in and ripping the case out of our hands. And you had better hope that court order comes in within the hour, because if it doesn't, this whole little debacle might just get leaked to the press. I can't imagine how embarrassing *that* publicity would be for you and all of Homeland Security, especially when they tie the story to the recent bioterrorist attack on New York City, and Homeland Security's failure to prevent it." *Shit.* I'm digging myself quite a hole if Siddiqui is working with Casilla, but I can't stop myself. "Now, call off your people, and let's just all wait for that court order, shall we?"

Siddiqui's face has turned stony. "You're making a big mistake, Detective."

"If I had a nickel for every time I've heard that...."

CHAPTER 8

"The world is reeling today after reports coming out of Rubezikan have suggested a sudden and unexplained forty percent WHISP conversion rate. As of this broadcast, there has been no official statement from President Pargulmahamadomet or the Rubezi government on the phenomenon and offers of assistance to help assess the situation by the UN have gone unanswered. Rubezikan was already on the Human Rights Watch list before it became the number one country on the WHISPs Rights Watch list in 2027 when foreign travel into and out of the country was suspended...." ~ CNN Report August 1st, 2029

"WELL, THAT WAS PRETTY AWESOME."

I flinch and a pen goes rolling off my desk.

"Whoa, easy there, Jumpy, it's just me." Crone sets a cup of coffee down next to my elbow. "Thought you could use this."

Picking up the pen off the floor, I sigh. "Thanks, but I'm not sure it was the right thing to do, and I'm pretty sure it's not going to make any difference in the long run. It doesn't seem like the feds are willing to work with the task force on this one."

"Maybe they were going to, but then you weren't here, and Siddiqui got a bug up her butt about it. Where were you, anyway?"

I pick up the coffee so I don't have to look at him. "Doctor's appointment."

He grunts. "Bad timing."

"Don't I know it." I take a sip, though the liquid's nuclear hot. "So, are we anywhere on anything?"

Crone leans against my desk and it gives an ominous creak. "Staties talked to the owner of the airfield. With a bit of persuasion, he confirmed the plane's destination was Rubezikan and that he was paid a boatload of cash to keep even the existence of the plane a secret."

"What do we know about the plane?"

Crone pulls out his phone. "Ah, the plane was a private jet, a Gulfstream V, up to nineteen passengers, ultra long range. When it landed, it was supposedly coming from Paris, but I don't think we've tracked down the airfield in France. Chances are, that was either a lie or they paid off the French airfield to keep the plane's departure off the records."

"Only nineteen passengers? How many people did we arrest at the lab?"

Crone just looks at me.

"Oh right, you weren't there." I dig into the case files on my laptop. "Five people arrested. Two taken in an ambulance that was intercepted before it reached the hospital, that's seven. Plus"—I take a deep breath—"plus Lincoln is eight. So, they could've had up to eleven others to get their people back and kidnap Lincoln. Dammit."

"What were you hoping?"

I lean back my head until my neck cracks. "I was hoping they had to leave some of their people behind."

"Ah." Crone continues to hover.

"Anything else?"

He slides his phone back into his pocket. "I think Green is still working with Tech on some things, but I'm not really sure what. Trying to track or hack something."

A thought from a previous conversation bobs to the surface of my brain. "You hear back anything from your contact in vice?"

"Just confirmation that there is a Rubezikani? Rubezi?"

I stare him down.

"Sorry. There is a presence here in the city, but it hasn't been around that long, and vice doesn't have anyone on the inside. According to the Serbians and Romanians, the Rubezikan group is very tightknit. They keep mostly to themselves and don't try to muscle in on anybody else's turf, but the rest of the syndicates are afraid of them and what their ultimate agenda is."

"Why don't they just take them out?"

Crone shrugs. "Too hard to pin them down. Plus, my buddy said any time they hit a Rubezikan target, they got hit back in a bad way, so they mainly leave them alone now."

"Where does their money come from? Drugs?"

"You'd think, but there's no evidence and that would make them more of a priority for vice. I think it's probably oil money."

This isn't helping anything. I rub my aching temples. "I thought you couldn't find Rubezikan on a map."

"I did some research since yesterday. Did you know—"

Clemont approaches Crone's side, eyes wide and impressed. "Shit, Harbinger, what did you say to Homeland Security earlier?"

"What do you mean? What's happening?"

He opens his mouth, but then spies something over my shoulder, slams it shut, and scurries off in the opposite direction like a spooked rabbit. I turn and Siddiqui is heading over to my desk, a frown etched on her professionally manicured face, and a single piece of paper in her hand. This is it. The court order came through. Casilla is my only hope now. Standing, I steel myself for her smug reproach. "Director Siddiqui, I take it that's—"

She gets much closer than I expect her to and I almost fall backward over my chair.

"I don't know what kind of connections you have," she hisses, "but your politicking better be worth your son's life." She thrusts the paper into my hands and turns on her black, patent heels. "Truman! Yee!"

Two of the other suited agents leap to attention and all but run to follow her toward the chief's former office.

"What the hell was that all about?" Crone's up and at my side.

"I have no idea." I stare down at the paper in my hands. It looks like a federal court order, and it takes a bit of skimming to see what Siddiqui is so pissed about. "Oh."

"What?" Crone leans over my shoulder. "What's the big...."

A few seconds pass as we both read and reread the order.

Then Crone grunts. "How the fuck did you manage that, Harbinger?"

The words on the paper gradually sinking in, I shake my head. "No idea."

CHAPTER 9

"Both the Organisation of Islamic Cooperation and the
Muslim World League have recently come forward to
condemn anti-WHISP movements within the Muslim
community. Their statements come just days after the
Vatican's announcement that it would hold a global
WHISP baptism. Though these statements of accep-
tance are encouraging, there still have been multiple
reports of local temples, mosques, and churches
refusing worshippers with WHISPs." ~ Excerpt New
York Times Article, *Religion and WHISPs*, October
3rd, 2027

"BEN?"

The apartment lights are on, and it isn't until just now I
realize that Ben hasn't called or texted to see what was up with
the feds. Maybe he was going through something similar at the
lab, so he didn't need to or didn't have time to call. Or maybe
he just left the lights on this morning in his haste to follow me.
"Ben?"

"In the kitchen."

I dump my coat, purse, and laptop on the threadbare coach,

then take off my sensible but still-not-comfortable heels and carry them down the hall. "Hey, you won't believe—"

Casilla is sitting at my kitchen table. My shoes hit the floor about the same time as my gun sights Casilla's forehead.

He grins. "Nice reflexes, Detective, but poor instincts."

I don't lower the gun. "I've had a long day."

"I know."

I look to Ben. Standing by the sink, he gives me a sad almost-smile, so I holster my gun. "What do you mean, 'you know'?"

Casilla motions to the other chair at the tiny table, but I stay standing. He shrugs. "Let's just say it was a necessary evil. I'm only sorry they sent Siddiqui. She's not easy to work with under the best circumstances."

Too many questions jostle for position in my sleep-deprived and addled brain to pick one out. Rubbing my forehead, I lean against the doorjamb for some kind of support. As if on cue, my stomach rumbles loudly.

Casilla chuckles and checks his watch. "Skip lunch again, Detective? I'd eat something if I were you, we don't have much time."

That focuses me. "Time before what?"

He pulls a face of surprise, though real or fake, I can't say. "Before our flight."

"Our flight?" My heart stutters in my chest. I look to Ben for confirmation.

Ben nods. "Casilla says we're going to Rubezikan."

The room spins. *I'm coming, Lincoln. Hang on. I'm coming.*

———

WE'RE IN AN SUV AND I'M TRYING TO CHOKE DOWN A protein bar. Sadly, there was no time for Ben to make eggs. The bite of peanutty grit goes down my throat like sandpaper.

"So, let me get this straight. You're the one who had Homeland Security swoop in and take the case away from the task force, and you're also the one who turned the court order into a mandate to work with the task force? I don't get it."

From the front passenger seat, Casilla shrugs. "It's all your fault really, Detective. Don't you think it would seem odd if you suddenly disappeared off a case involving your son? Now, with the help of a little convenient theatrics, it looks like your dispute with Siddiqui got you reassigned. But I knew you wouldn't give up without a fight, so I gift-wrapped that last part about Homeland Security cooperating with the task force. You're welcome, by the way. Hopefully, by the time anyone thinks to question what happened, we'll be back in the U.S. with your son."

"You think it'll be that quick?" I hate the hope in my voice. I'm getting Lincoln back no matter how long it takes.

"Let's hope so, Detective."

Ben's been silent most of the trip, so I reach over and squeeze his hand. "You okay?"

He gives me a grim smile and a half-nod, but he knows I know him better than that.

"You don't have to do this."

He frowns until he wrinkles and looks away. "Of course, I do. It's not that." His eyes meet mine again. "It's...." He swallows hard, glances at Casilla, then back at me, then pointedly at my stomach.

I shake my head just enough so that Ben sees it. "Don't worry about that."

Her.

Shut up, Liv. "We have to focus on Lincoln right now."

"So, I meant to ask you before...."

Both Ben and I jerk our heads toward Casilla's voice.

"Can it do any tricks?"

"What?"

"Your WHISP. Can it do anything useful? Maybe fly around and kill people. That'd be helpful to know."

I open my mouth and Ben squeezes my hand. I catch Ben's eye. He's right. Casilla probably doesn't know the whole story about Chester. Probably doesn't know about my recent visit to Kirby. Doesn't know how deep his flippant remark cuts. "Not that I know of."

"Bummer. Are you sure? Have you really tried? Could be an important resource for us."

I'm an important resource.

You're the reason Lincoln is being held by terrorists in Rubezikan. "I—"

"You, Particle Physicist, isn't there any way you could like boost her signal? Make her have a super WHISP?"

Ben glances at me, his eyes filled with confusion and doubt, but also spinning gears. I know that look. He's thought about it. Of course, he has. It's his job to analyze WHISPs: what they're made of, what causes them, what could unmake them, what could make them stronger. What if I could find a way to use Liv to save Lincoln other than simply curing him from the WHISP virus?

"Experimenting on human WHISPs is illegal," Ben's voice is like a wound piano string.

"Technically, but a lot of what we're about to do could be considered illegal. Personally, I've never had much use for that word. I prefer to think in terms of right and wrong."

Ben's face darkens. "And you don't think it's wrong to experiment on humans?"

If Casilla realizes he's hit a nerve, he doesn't care. "Drug companies do it all the time, experimental drug trials and what-not. If it's for the greater good, then what's the harm?"

"I think the victims of the Tuskegee experiment would believe differently."

Casilla makes a dismissive gesture with his hand. "I'm not

some kind of monster, I'm talking about experiments with informed consent."

Ben's still bristling. "We don't know enough about WHISPs to make any consent informed."

Finally, Casilla shifts in his seat to look at Ben. "There's risk in everything, Doctor. As long as the participants know there's a risk and accept that risk, then it's all for the greater good. Isn't it?"

"Sure, whatever you say."

Ben squeezes my hand again, looking for solidarity, but my gaze is locked on Casilla. He's talking about saving Lincoln. He's asking how far we're willing to go to save Lincoln, if Ben's willing to experiment on me and Liv. That's why he brought Ben along in all this.

I face Ben. "I know the risks."

"What?"

"Ben, if it could save Lincoln, if we could find a way to use Liv to save him, why wouldn't we do that?"

"Because it could"—he takes a deep breath—"it could *damage* you, Sylvy."

"Isn't that my choice?"

He shakes his head, his eyes red and shimmering. "I could end up losing you both. I could lose...everything."

I grip his hand in both of mine. "If we lose Lincoln, you *will* lose us both." It will destroy me. I know it will. And deep down, Ben knows it will, too.

CHAPTER 10

"WHISPs are an abomination, an affront to Allah. We are at the dawn of a new jihad. If we do not eradicate the darkness around us, how can we ever hope to vanquish the darkness within us? I call upon every citizen to cleanse our communities of this scourge...." ~ Excerpt Presidential Address by President Pargulmahamadomet January 20, 2027

I'VE NEVER BEEN ON A PRIVATE JET BEFORE, BUT THE novelty and opulence are lost on me as I watch Ben go over calculations on his laptop and I sneak a 600 mg Ibuprofen for my aching elbow. He's working on using a similar system to the one he developed to help stop the WHISP virus to try to boost Liv's abilities. I try not to think about the pain and the fact that Ben's system almost killed us. *Me. Us. Whatever.*

Unable to sit still any longer but unwilling to bother Ben, I rise and deposit myself across from Casilla. Though the words tear my throat, I have to ask the question that's burning a hole in my heart, "What are the odds my son's still alive, at this point?"

Casilla looks up from his laptop, his face wry. "Pretty good, actually."

"But it's been days. And we won't even get there for another"—I tax my brain trying to compute flight time, ground time, and time zones—"another twenty-four hours?"

"Only about twenty-two, if all goes well."

"That's forever in a kidnapping case."

Casilla sighs and closes his laptop. "I'm sure you realize this isn't a normal kidnapping."

"He's just another test subject."

Casilla's eyebrow hitches up and he gulps the rest of his drink, a gin and tonic by the clarity and lemon twist. "How much do you know about the WHISP situation in Rubezikan?"

"Not much," I admit. "Just that there's been a lot on the news about human rights violations against WHISPers there."

"Well yes, but there's more to it than that."

"Like what?"

"Like about forty-four percent of the population there, mainly the poorest people, have a WHISP."

My eyebrows reach for my hairline. "Forty-four percent? That's crazy. I didn't think they were more tech-crazy than Japan."

He shakes his head. "They're not. In fact, the majority of their citizens have absolutely no access to computers or the internet. You're not in a need-to-know position right now, so let's just say that their government—and by government, I mean crazy, egotistical, dictator asshole—was testing something on his people a while back and the result of that was roughly forty-four percent of the population forming a WHISP overnight."

"Overnight?"

"You can understand how an isolated population not privy to the worldwide WHISP phenomenon might go a little apeshit if something like that happened. It would seem like the apocalypse or rapture or something."

Brain whirling, I rub my chin. "So, the government who caused the WHISPs had to turn around and act like they were 'protecting' their people from WHISPs to avoid widespread panic and anarchy."

Casilla makes a dismissive gesture. "Basically."

I shake my head. Doesn't matter. What matters is Lincoln. "How does this add up to Lincoln still being alive?"

"Well, they certainly don't need another test subject. Plenty of their own people for that. Best guess is that they took him as an informational resource. He's on the WHISP Task Force, and he was going over papers from the lab when they took him. It's likely they figured he was a valuable asset to have a WHISP and still be sent out to go over records at a site known to be testing a WHISP virus."

"I didn't think of that." Come to think of it, I'm pissed off now that Ben let him go to the lab site. But I have to reign in my anger. I can't start blaming Ben for what happened. Not now.

"Don't feel bad. I've been doing this a hell of a lot longer than you have."

This gets my hackles up. I've been a cop almost thirty years now and a detective more than twenty. I should've seen the terrorist's intentions with Lincoln. *Shake it off, Harbinger. Hindsight is twenty-twenty. Focus.* "So, what's the plan on the ground?"

"We'll land in Uzbekistan and make our way across the border by camel, then...."

My scowl stops him.

"Sorry, just trying to lighten the mood a little." He clears his throat. "We'll land in Uzbekistan then drive across the border and meet with our contacts in Rubezikan to see what they know about where the terrorist group may be heading."

What? My mind flashes to the last map I examined of

Rubezikan. A vast country larger than California. "Don't you have spy satellites or something that tracked the plane?"

Casilla fixes me with a long-suffering glare. "It's not that eas—"

My cell buzzes and I pull it from my pocket. It's a text from Crone: Where are you? Before I can answer, Casilla snatches the phone from my hand and deftly removes the sim card.

"What the hell, Harbinger?"

It occurs to me now that I should've put it on airplane mode, but it wasn't as if the stewardesses gave us a safety briefing before takeoff. "Sorry, I didn't think to shut it off."

His exasperation is not quenched. "Why did you even bring it?"

I shrug. Open my mouth, then close it, remembering movies like *The Bourne Identity*. "Sorry, I thought you'd have told us what was and wasn't safe to bring."

The red in Casilla's face darkens as he gets up and makes his way to another agent, a blonde woman of probable Nordic descent, a few seats away. "Nichterson, clone this, then bag the original, and do the same if the doctor still has his cell." When he returns to his seat, Casilla's face is a shade less red. "You're right. I didn't say anything. I haven't worked with real civilians in a while."

Silence stretches between us like a veil until Nichterson returns with a squat, grey, utilitarian cell phone and hands it to me. "Use that. It's a clone of your phone, but the signal won't be traceable."

I turn it over in my hands. "Really? How does that work?"

"Well, the signal—"

"It's complicated. Thanks, Nichterson." Casilla dismisses her with a nod.

She shrugs and walks toward Ben, seated at the back of the plane.

I turn on the phone and an ugly replication of my home screen appears minus a few apps.

"Sorry, you won't be able to record your steps with that phone. Or make restaurant reservations."

I go to Crone's text. "My colleague's asking where I am. Is there some official CIA response you want me to use?"

"Tell him Homeland Security reassigned you to Washington for a few days to give you a debriefing there. Also tell him there's a lot of security and you won't always have access to your cell."

As I shoot off an appropriate text, I wonder if Crone will buy one word of it. I try to think of other loose ends, but with Grumps the Cat already in Naomi's care, I can't really think of any, so I pocket the phone and return my gaze to Casilla. "So, we land, cross the border, make contact, then what?"

Casilla leans back in his seat and closes his eyes. "Then we get your boy back."

CHAPTER 11

Excerpt Personal Diary: Dr. Ahmed Mahadow
Friday, August 17th, 2029
"The team here in New York is now up to 17 members from my own lab and a growing number of CIA scientists, yet the work remains static with fewer WHISP subjects to perform tests on. Many of the test subjects we are presented with are also drugged which skews results and makes the testing more difficult. Requests for additional, non-drugged subjects have gone unanswered as have requests for moving the operation back to Yedys."

I STARE AT CASILLA'S SERENE FACE FOR A WHILE, wishing I was confident enough to sleep, then scan the cabin to see if there's anyone else still awake I could grill for more details, or maybe just to introduce myself and get a sense of who the rest of our team is. My gaze finds a dark-haired, bronze-skinned man a little younger than Casilla, in his mid-thirties, is my guess, reading a book a few rows up. After grabbing a bottled water from the station just behind Casilla, I head over and casually drop into the seat across from him.

"You guys always travel so stylishly?"

The man with irises the color of black coffee looks up from the book, *A Gentleman in Moscow* by Amor Towles. "Not usually. Typically, we're in the cargo hold of a C-12 or C-37, but I guess this is all they had on such short notice."

"Must be a nice change of pace."

He shrugs. "Think I'd prefer the C-12. Doesn't really feel like a mission this way."

Shaking off the heat rising in my throat because he feels like finding my son isn't a real mission, I extend my hand. "Detective Sylvia Harbinger."

He grasps it, "Manganaro"—a slight pause—"TJ, but we usually just go by last names on a mission."

When he releases my hand, I nod. "Sure." He seems about to go back to reading, so I rush on, "You been with the CIA long?"

He gives me a look. "We don't really do this before a mission."

"Do what?"

"Chit chat. Get to know one another better. It makes things easier."

From his grim expression, I don't have to ask what kinds of things it makes easier: watching people die, sacrificing them, leaving them behind in enemy territory.

"Right. So, what do I need to know about you, mission-wise?"

"I've been to Rubezikan three times, I'm good with bombs, and I'm a better shot than Casilla."

His last comment raises my eyebrows. "You've worked with Casilla before?"

Manganaro nods toward another agent stretched out over two seats of the middle row near the front of the plane, apparently asleep. "And Onai."

"So, what do I need to know about Casilla?"

He snorts. "You've met him, right?"

I smile. "As advertised?"

"As advertised."

I hitch a thumb toward the lounging man. "And Onai?"

Manganaro shrugs. "Very quiet. Very professional. Gets the job done, but don't expect any extraneous conversation."

"Got it. What about," I strain to recall pre-boarding introductions, "Valcross?"

"Don't know him personally, but there're rumors he once saved Casilla's life."

I mull that over a moment. It seems like an odd thing to say. "Doesn't that happen a lot in your line of work? Saving your fellow agent's lives?"

"It shouldn't."

I raise my eyebrows.

"I don't mean it like that. I mean, a mission shouldn't go to shit enough that you have to, and if they do, usually no one makes it out."

"I see." I try to steer the conversation away from that cheery thought. "Any idea about the others on the team?"

"The ones we're meeting on the ground? Sorry, no."

The conversation stalls again, and I can't take the silence. "So, just how pissed off were you when you heard civilians were tagging along?"

"Well"—he points to my holster—"you're not exactly a civilian."

Suddenly, I realize that Manganaro's eyes haven't once strayed to Liv and the words are out of my mouth before I can swallow them back, "I'm not exactly a whimp either."

His face clouds with confusion. "A wimp?"

I point over my shoulder at Liv. "Sorry, it means non-WHISPer."

His expression smooths and he finally looks at Liv. "Oh, that. It's not like I've never seen one before, Detective."

"And you don't think it's a hindrance to the mission?"

A soberness creeps into his voice. "Honestly? You'd have stuck out even without it, but this isn't an infiltration mission, and we're not trying to get you to pass for anything you're not. If all goes well, no one will ever see us, so it doesn't matter." He opens his mouth again, but then closes it.

"What?"

"It's just...you're a cop and you don't seem like the type who spends every spare moment in front of a computer playing WarCraft or something, and you're on the older side of most WHISPers...."

As he trails off, his question becomes clear. "You want to know how I got Li—it."

"Yeah, sorry. Probably a pretty rude question."

"Particle accelerator."

"Oh."

———

WHEN I FINALLY LEAVE MANGANARO TO HIS BOOK and wander to the aft of the cabin, I find Valcross helping Ben with the WHISP amplifier.

"Hey, how's it going?"

Ben wipes the back of his arm across his sweaty forehead. Dark rings have settled under his eyes. "Great, considering I don't know what the hell I'm doing, and I could kill you if I get it wrong."

Valcross shakes his head. "Very unlikely. CIA worked years to find magic kill frequency and no luck."

I'm surprised by his thick Russian, or maybe Ukrainian, accent, but then again, it's not like Onai, Casilla, and Manganaro are all-American, Iowa-raised farm boys, either.

Ben sighs. "Yeah, but they didn't have to worry about disrupting WHISP particles."

Valcross shrugs. "You are expert."

The screwdriver in Ben's hand slips off the machine and tumbles to the floor. "Shit!"

I put my hand on his shoulder. "Maybe you should take a break."

"Da, come, there are sandwiches." Valcross nods to Ben.

As we follow him to the refreshment station, I'm itching to ask Valcross about saving Casilla's life, but not having any idea of the circumstances, I decide it's better not to dredge up a possibly traumatic memory right before the mission. *The mission. Lincoln.* My stomach twists, but not as painfully as it would've a few hours ago. I glance around the cabin. These are good men. Professionals. *Sit tight, kiddo, help is on the way.*

CHAPTER 12

Recovered File CAW Server
Date: Unknown
Subject: Henderson, Brian
Test: WHISP Separation Trial
Subject was separated from WHISP via placement in a
Faraday cage for one hour. Subject complained of
headache and nausea, but WHISP remained seemingly
unaffected. However, a reversal of the test with placement of WHISP within the Faraday cage yielded much
more promising results in terms of permanent WHISP
removal, though effects on the subject were much more
severe.

My teeth clack together in an alarming
manner as the truck bumps over another huge rut. Teetering on
the edge of exhaustion, only the rough road is keeping me
awake. I know I should've slept on the plane, but I couldn't
keep images of Lincoln being tortured out of my mind.

We crossed the Rubezikan border in the night without inci-
dent and all I could think was that I was closer to Lincoln than

I'd been in days. I'd wanted to try Ben's WHISP amplifier to use Liv to find him or feel for his presence or something, but despite working on it for almost the entire twenty-two-hour flight, he said it wasn't ready for use. I sensed he was stalling, but didn't pressure him, since there wasn't much time before we boarded the truck. One truck. Eight people, now that Agent Hardja, a coffee-skinned man who never smiles, and Jones, a tan, sandy-haired agent even younger than Manganaro, have joined us. Casilla had assured me we'd meet additional forces once on the ground, but I guess I'd expected a much bigger response.

My cloned cell buzzes in my pocket and I just manage to pull it out without dropping it, but I do bang my bad elbow on the wall of the truck as I'm jostled nearly off the truck's metal bench. "Ow, fuck!"

"You okay?" Ben grabs my arm to steady me.

"Yeah, just bashed my elbow." I blink back tears of pain.

He points to the phone. "Crone again?"

I check the screen and nod. "About every four hours."

"Any progress?"

I nod. "A little. Tech's been working around the clock with some specialists from Homeland Security and they've been able to retrieve a little data from the lab computers."

"That's great. What did they find?"

"Well, not so great, actually. They think the lab was just a small piece of a bigger agenda. Maybe even a distraction."

Ben blinks. "Shit."

"Yeah."

The truck goes over another obstacle and Ben's head hits the ceiling.

"Shit!" He rubs his head with one hand and holds on to the bench with the other.

I can't help but notice Casilla grinning next to Ben.

"How much farther?" my words are almost lost in a sudden roar of the truck's engine as we screech to a halt. My relief turns sour as Casilla, Hardja, Onai, and Manganaro pull their guns and rush to the canvas serving as the back door.

"What's—"

I put a finger to Ben's lips as I pull my own gun and motion for him to get under the bench.

After the cacophony of the drive, the eerie and unnatural silence chills my blood despite the dry, desert heat. I look to Casilla for direction, but he and the other agents ignore me. I scan the interior of the truck, but other than a hatch on the ceiling and the back-canvas flap, there's no way out. If something's wrong, and my keen cop sense is telling me something's wrong, we're sitting ducks. Someone outside shouts and I tense, releasing the safety on my gun and crouching next to where Ben is crammed beneath the metal bench. I can't understand anything being said, so I watch Casilla and Hardja's faces for their responses. The voice might be angry, but the raised voice might also indicate someone trying to make themselves heard.

The response to the shouting is much softer, so I can't tell if there's fear there. A bead of sweat meanders down my nose and drips onto my knee. Another bead falls from my eyebrow onto the lashes of my right eye. Resisting the urge to wipe my face, I blink carefully so only some of the sweat stings my eye. Casilla and the others haven't moved. If gunfire erupts, I'll drop on my stomach and crawl toward the flap.

Laughter erupts, gruff and throaty.

Casilla's shoulders relax, but he doesn't holster his weapon or retake his seat until the truck starts up again and slowly resumes its grinding journey. Safety reengaged, I holster my gun and help Ben out from under the bench. "What the hell was that?"

Casilla shrugs. "New tariff."

"What?"

He sighs. "A bribe, Detective. These back roads are always riddled with 'officials' ready to check your papers and fine or delay the uncooperative."

"Or just kill you and take whatever you're transporting," Hardja chimes in.

"Or that." Casilla nods.

Ben swallows hard. "So, we got lucky?"

Casilla shakes his head. "No. Lucky would've been not running into anyone. There's no guarantee this guy won't have a roadblock waiting for us in a few miles. It's hard to tell which ones are actually officials and which are just thugs." He pulls a radio from his belt. "Jones, status."

The radio crackles to life a few seconds later. "No insignia on the uniform. Gave him thirty-five hundred manat. Seemed happy."

"Good. But eyes open, Jones."

"Always are."

Casilla clips the radio back onto his belt. "Probably a thug. Only took a thousand US. Real officials usually ask for five thousand or more."

"What do you want me to do if it happens again?"

Casilla raises an eyebrow. "Keep quiet. Try not to get shot." He takes a drink from a canteen, then looks at me again, his eyes focusing over my shoulder. "And stay away from the walls."

Anger burns like a road flare in my chest. *Away from the walls?* Then fizzles... Oh. Liv. If they spot a WHISP outside the truck they'll probably start shooting. I didn't think of that. Ben gives me an I'm-sorry-Babe look before another rough patch of road tears his gaze away.

Liv, you better start earning your keep, because right now you're just pissing me off. I feel a phantom hand on my stomach. "Stop that."

"What?" Ben's looking at me again, and I realize I've spoken the last part out loud.

"Nothing."

CHAPTER 13

Excerpt USCIS Internal Memo
Monday, April 20, 2026
Re: WHISP Immigration
Additionally, the refugee status of the person or persons must be taken into account with respect to policies and prejudices regarding WHISPs in the country of origin.

WHEN WE STOP AGAIN, CASILLA IS MUCH MORE relaxed. "We're here."

Beat up from the truck ride and tired beyond words, I still manage a weak, "Where's here?"

"Bez Imeni." He smiles, but when neither I nor Ben respond, the smile wanders away from his lips. "Neither of you took Russian in school, I take it."

"About all I know is kalashnikov, pakhan, and politsiya."

"It means the town with no name."

"Okay."

He throws back the canvas and jumps out of the truck then turns back and extends a hand to me. "It's a refuge for many persecuted Rubezi."

I glance at his hand then jump down beside him without

taking it. "So, what, you promise them the freedoms of America if they help you?"

"No. Mostly they help us just because they hate their own government. He nods to a man walking up to the back of the truck with a lantern.

The man smiles. "That and the money."

When he reaches Casilla, the two men embrace. Then Casilla pulls out a wad of bills and hands it to the man, who sets down the lantern, makes a perfunctory check of the currency, then pockets the cash.

Casilla turns back to me. "Detective, this is Ikhlosbek."

The man nods and extends his hand, but then his eyes widen and he draws it back sharply and says something in Rubezi to Casilla. Casilla raises his hands in a placating gesture and replies slowly in Rubezi. Ikholosbek scowls and glances around, picks up the lantern, then motions me to follow him as he turns away.

I look to Casilla. "What's going on?"

Casilla shrugs. "Sorry, it's your WHISP. Some of the folks around here are tolerant of them, but some, not so much. Better go with Ikhlosbek for now so we don't run into trouble." He looks away. "Hardja. Go with her. Make sure nobody freaks out."

Hardja and I follow Ikhlosbek down an alley between lopsided, dusty stone buildings and then through a colorless wooden door in the side of one. Inside, stone steps lead down and Ikhlosbek continues without pausing. I glance back toward the truck where I left Ben struggling with his equipment, but it's hidden around a bend in the crooked alley.

The steps are slick with sand and lack a handrail, making them fairly treacherous, but fortunately, it isn't long before we reach the bottom and enter an underground room. Ikhlosbek flips a switch and several naked bulbs hanging from wires along the ceiling come to life. In one corner is a kitchenette with a refrigerator hooked up to a small generator and a rickety wooden table with four chairs. In another corner is a worn couch. Most of the rest of the room is taken up by electrical equipment piled high on several desks shoved together.

Ikhlosbek turns to us but doesn't meet my eye. He points to a door across from the stairs. "Bathroom." Then he practically runs back up the stairs. I glance at Hardja, but he's already headed over to the desks and switching things on, so I decide to use the facilities before everyone gets there. I cross to the bathroom, open the door, flip a switch, and find a bucket and a basin. I sigh. At least there's a door and a light.

———

A VAST DESERT STRETCHES OUT BEFORE ME IN EVERY direction. Illuminated only by a pale moon, long shadows stretch out from the dark dunes. The hair on my arms prickles as the shadows begin to flow and writhe. I want to run, but there's nowhere to go. Around me, the shadows coalesce into the outlines of thousands of people, an army of WHISPs. As one, they reach toward me, empty sockets staring, empty mouths yawning in silent screams. "Help me, Liv." But as soon as I speak, I know she's gone. I'm alone. Phantom arms grip me. I start to scream, but a hundred hands cover my mouth. I can't move. I can't breathe. Inside my abdomen, something stirs.

"Sylvy."

My eyes fly open and Ben is shaking me gently. I rocket upright and hit my head on the bunk above me. Even as stars flood my vision, I try to stand. "What's happening? Is it time?"

Ben tightens his hold on my arms and prevents me from standing. "No, nothing. God I'm sorry. I didn't mean to scare you. I just thought you might want to eat something."

As drowsiness melts away, the pain in my head cuts

through and throbs. I rub the top of my head, but that only sharpens the pain.

"Are you okay?"

"I'm fine." Those words have never meant less than they do right now. "Have they heard anything yet?"

"Not yet. Casilla says it may take another couple hours for the scouts to report in."

"Hours?" The waiting, imagining every horror the terrorists could be visiting on my son, brings bile to the back of my throat.

"Here, I brought you some bread and cheese." Ben proffers a plate with some flat, brown bread on it and a small hunk of off-white cheese.

The sight of the food makes my stomach turn in on itself. "I can't." I shake my head and the throbbing returns.

"Sylvy. You have to eat something."

"I ate on the plane."

"No, you didn't. Now come on." He picks up the bread, folds it, and dips his hand down and then up again. "Don't force me to make airplane noises."

The frown on my lips cracks but doesn't quite become a smile. I take the bread, tear off a small piece, and put it in my mouth. A cross between pita bread and naan with herbs I don't recognize, it's surprisingly flavorful for its simplicity. Before I know it, I've eaten the whole piece. Ben picks up the cheese, and grudgingly, I take it from him. I glance around the bunkroom, lit only by a single yellow bulb. One of the other bunks on the far side is occupied and I feel guilty for making noise. I point to the bed and motion Ben to head to the door. I follow him out into the main room and find most of the agents lounging on the couch or playing cards at the table. Casilla sits at the desk with the equipment, but he's leaning back with his eyes closed. Though I know we don't even know where Lincoln is being held yet, anger bubbles under my skin. Shouldn't they be doing something productive?

Ben takes the plate over to the kitchenette and washes it in the sink while I look for a place to sit. No wonder Ben brought the food into the bunkroom. My throat tightens as the room closes in around me. Breathing heavily, I head for the stairs. A blur materializes next to me and someone grabs my arm. Instincts and training kicking in, I twist away and bring my too stiff elbow up into thin air where a chin should've been.

"Hah, almost forgot you were a cop." Casilla is grinning as he steps in front of the stairs. "You going somewhere?"

I keep a fighting stance. "I just wanted to go upstairs and get some air."

"I don't think that's the best idea."

The urge to punch Casilla is strong, but I force myself to relax. "I wasn't going to leave, just sit and breathe at the top of the stairs."

Ben slides in beside me. "It is a little crowded down here. I'll go with her."

Casilla's eye roll is practically audible, but he concedes. "Fine, but don't open the door. Seriously, we're trying to lay low here and I'll see if you do." He points to one of the screens on the desk with a video feed of the door.

"Fine." I brush past him and try not to kill myself rushing up the worn steps. Ben's footsteps are several feet behind me. Probably making room for Liv. At the top, the air is hot and not even a little refreshing, but the sunlight peeking through the door is a welcome change from the gloom of the underground rooms. I let Ben reach the top then turn and sit on the first step.

He joins me. "You okay?"

I open my mouth, then close it when no words come and shrug. The phone in my pocket buzzes against my hip and I twitch. Since it didn't have a signal underground, I'd forgotten it was even on. I pull it out and see another text from Crone.

Crone: Having fun in Washington?

I've been ignoring all his texts since I sent the message about being reassigned, but replying to this one seems better than just sitting here, so I do.

Harbinger: Not really. Lots of meetings. Any news?

Crone: I want to play poker with you sometime.

Harbinger: Come again?

Crone: You're a terrible liar for a cop.

I chew my bottom lip. I should've answered one of his texts before now. Shit.

Harbinger: I don't kn— Before I finish typing, another text pops up.

Crone: Where R U?

CHAPTER 14

Excerpt Personal Diary: Dr. Ahmed Mahadow
Thursday, September 6th, 2029
"I've not heard back from Dr. Abdullayev in several
weeks. I'm beginning to suspect my communications
with him have not been getting through. Though
nothing has been officially said, we haven't been away
from the compound in six weeks, and I'm not sure what
would happen if we tried to leave."

BEN ISN'T EXACTLY LOOKING OVER MY SHOULDER,
but with him sitting right next to me, I can't hide my distress.
"What is it?"
I meet his eye. "It's Crone."
"I figured. Did they find something?"
"Not exactly." I return my attention to my cell screen.
Harbinger: Finding my son.
Crone: Figured. Can I help?
Harbinger: Keep on the down low. Keep Homeland from
fucking up the investigation and keep the task force going.
Crone: Is that all?
Harbinger: Keep me in the loop.

Crone: Like you did with me?

Harbinger: Hey. I answered your text didn't I?

Crone: *Emoji with tongue sticking out.*

I stick the phone back in my pocket.

"Well?" Ben's staring at me.

I almost forget that he's as starved for information and leads as I am. "Crone knows I'm not in Washington."

Ben deflates slightly. "Oh. Does that matter?"

I shrug. "Well, it's easier not to have to ignore and lie to him."

"I dunno. Gives you something to do."

"Speaking of which, shouldn't you be working on your amplification equipment?"

Ben looks away. "I'm finished with it."

"Thought so." I stand and brush off sand in a futile effort before starting down the stairs.

Ben gets up, too. "Where're you going?"

I don't turn. "We should be testing it."

"Sylvy, I...."

I'm not sure what he says after that because an explosion rocks the shelter and turns the rickety bunker door to splinters behind me.

———

FACEDOWN ON THE STAIRS, I'M SLIDING DOWN while booted feet are running up. There's shouting, some automatic gunfire. I try to breathe deep, but get a lungful of dust and am coughing more than breathing. I get my arms under me, but gravity, the steep steps, and my throbbing bad elbow keep me prone. No matter. Soon I'm in a heap at the bottom. The sunlight from the now gaping hole at the top of the stairs is lighting up the dust in a blinding display like a small nebula. I can't see anything in the stairwell. I can't see Ben. Oh god. Ben was still at the top of the steps.

"Ben?" my voice is a croak I'm not sure I can hear outside my own head. I try again. "Ben?"

Someone emerges from the dust and, at first, I think it's Ben, but it's Casilla. "Come on. We've gotta move."

I think he's going to help me up, but instead he rushes past me into the room. My ears are ringing, but through the swirling dust, I watch him load equipment and guns into a duffle bag. What should I be gathering? *Ben.* I don't trust myself to stand, but I twist my body and crawl up the stairs. There's still some gunfire, but not as much. My hands run into something soft, wet. Hair. Ben's head covered in blood. Everything stops. He groans, stirs, and the world roars to life again. Suddenly, I'm terrified that Casilla will leave Ben behind if he's too injured. I have to get Ben up.

"Ben. Get up. We have to go." Dust fills my mouth and coats my tongue with a muddy paste. I push on his shoulders, trying to get him to sit up.

"What happened?"

His voice is such a relief, I sag as a sob tears through me. Then a strong hand grabs my shoulder and hauls me to my feet, pulling me up toward the light.

"No, no, he's still alive! Ben's okay! Don't leave him!" I'm vaguely aware that I'm screaming and pawing at the hand on my shoulder. Another clamps over my mouth.

"Easy. I know. We won't leave him. Shut up."

But I don't believe him. I gouge the hand clenching my shoulder with my nails and drop to my knees at the same time. The hand releases and I fall next to Ben. Muffled curses trail behind me. I've got my arms around Ben and I'm lifting, trying to get him up, trying to get him to stand. At first, he's dead weight. No. Please no. But then his body stiffens, his arms return my embrace, and together we're standing. Then my foot slips, and we're both going down before someone catches me under my arm, pulls me up to the landing, then shoves Ben and I back against one crumbling wall.

Casilla peers around the hole where the door used to be then at me. "Can he run?"

I don't consult Ben. "We'll be right behind you."

Clearly not the answer he was looking for, Casilla bares his teeth in response, then holds up his fingers and counts down from five. I'm considering my chances if I have to drag Ben. He seems steady on his feet right now, but his head and face are covered with blood and sand, so I can't see his expression and he hasn't spoken since he asked what happened. I can't do any more evaluation though because Casilla drops his last finger and we're on the move. Diving out from the shelter of the doorway, I expect gunfire, but the alley is eerily quiet and seemingly abandoned. Where are the other members of the team or squad or whatever? I don't see Hardja or any of the others or the truck. Ben is holding his own, but he's still leaning on me enough that our progress is slow. We're losing ground on Casilla despite the fact that he's carrying a duffle bag full of guns and surveillance equipment. My heart is thundering in my chest and rushing blood deafens my already ringing ears, so when the gunfire starts up again, I've no idea from what direction it's coming until shards of clay hit my back from a near miss.

Falling more than taking cover, I aim toward a break in the wall on my right hoping it's not hiding more shooters. Blissfully, the opening is nothing more than an alcove and it's empty. After returning fire, Casilla backtracks and rejoins us. "We've got additional fire from the east. The doc's ragged, you'll have to come to us. About 100 feet west of the door—"

Gunfire chips away at the edge of our hiding spot and Casilla has to stop reporting and return fire again. I set Ben down behind me, pull my gun, and join him. He only pauses a moment then nods at me. "Aim high. Snipers."

I nod and reposition to try to get eyes on my targets on the rooftops. At the same time, my mind is reeling. How could snipers miss us in a narrow alley? But there's still a lot of sand and dust in the air from the blast. I can't see much, either. I try to judge the angle of the gouges in the wall and fire a few more shots back. Another volley makes me duck back and press against Ben. He's still warm, though that could just be the ambient heat. I'd be dripping with sweat if the dust wasn't turning my sweat to mud. Thinking about the heat is making it a hundred times worse and suddenly I'm roasting in my own skin. *Keep it together.*

There's a roar and a shadow falls over the alcove as a truck screeches to a stop in front of us. It's not our original truck, but I don't care at all, at this point. I have to assume it's our rescue, because if it's not, we're dead. I holster my gun because I need both hands to get Ben up and don't want to accidentally shoot him. Casilla catches my eye then nods and lays down a barrage of cover fire while Ben and I scramble to the back of the truck. Hardja and Manganaro are waiting and drag us up into the back while scanning behind. I turn to assist Casilla, but he doesn't follow. The truck roars into gear and Hardja and Manganaro jump in. I grab Manganaro's arm. "Where's Casilla?"

He shakes me off and doesn't answer.

CHAPTER 15

Excerpt Homeland Security Internal Memo
Date Redacted
Re: Terrorist Activity New York
...have been aware of a growing concern in New York for
several months and have been working closely with the
Bureau of Counterterrorism to gain intelligence and
coordinate efforts to stop any known terrorist activities.
Whether these activities are WHISP-centered or WHISP-
related is thus far unclear.

"I thought you said Bez Imeni was safe."

"I never said that." Casilla uses a splash of water from his
canteen to wash the dirt off his face.

We're camped under a large, rocky outcrop with desert in all
directions. After driving for over four hours, I can finally hear
without a funny tinny quality to the sound, but the rays of the
sinking sun are splitting my head open like a ripe cantaloupe. I
rub at the grime on my own face then press my temples

between my thumb and forefinger and close my eyes. "What the hell happened back there?"

"Here." Casilla nudges my arm.

I open my eyes and find two white tablets on his palm. "Cyanide?"

"Aspirin."

I take the pills from him and send them down my sore throat with a swallow of water.

"How's he doing?"

Ben. My tear ducts prickle, but I force a laugh. "He's fine. My husband's super lucky he's a klutz."

Confusion clouds Casilla's face. "Come again?"

"He slipped on the stairs and fell right before the explosion. If he'd been standing up..." *He'd be dead.*

"Oh." Casilla fails to suppress a smile. Then fails to suppress a chuckle.

A well of grave humor threatens a laugh, but then I remember why we're here. They wouldn't scrap the mission because of this, would they? I clear my throat. "What now? Do you think the attack has something to do with the terrorists?"

Casilla shakes his head. "They'd have no way of knowing we even knew where they were headed, so no."

"But you were trying to find them. You sent scouts or informants or whatever to gather information, to ask questions."

"And none of them would've led anyone back to that bunker."

"Then what happened?" And does it change anything?

Casilla shrugs. "Best guess? That 'official' we met on the road guessed where we were going and sold us out to actual government or just bigger, more organized thugs, hoping for a big payday, or..."

"Or what?"

He doesn't look at me. "Nothing."

"Tell me."

He looks up and lets out a breath. "Could've been that somebody saw you when we came in."

"Saw *me*?"

"Saw your WHISP, Harbinger, your WHISP. For fuck sake, do you really forget about it that easily? Don't you like feel it or something?"

Since the explosion, I hadn't spared a single thought for Liv. "They blew us up because of Liv?" Shit. I hadn't meant to say Liv, it just came out, but Casilla doesn't give any indication that he noticed I gave her a name.

"Maybe not. But people react funny to WHISPs over here. Sometimes they think they're contagious. Sometimes they shoot at them. They don't understand them like we do."

I snort at that. "Yeah, right. Like we understand them. If there's anything I've learned on the task force, it's that we don't fully understand WHISPs."

Exasperation floods Casilla's face. "You know what I mean."

Pain echoes in my chest when I breathe. "Well, what now?" Please don't tell me Liv ruined everything.

"Now we regroup. Intel came in a little before the bomb. We think they might be holding Lincoln in Yedys."

"Where's that?"

"It's a prison camp close to the Amu Darya River."

My heart splinters. "A prison camp?"

Casilla nods. "We think there's also a lab there. Word is there's been extensive construction and renovations though the actual prison population has remained stable. Also, there's been a lot of shipments lately that the guards haven't opened, that just go away."

"So, we're headed there now?"

Casilla shakes his head. "We need to set up a new base of operations first."

"You have more hideouts in towns with no name?"

"A few. We're waiting for confirmation that the road's clear first."

I look at the emptiness around us. "Confirmation from whom?"

He shrugs and glances up.

The sky above is cloudless, so I wonder if he means a satellite, but I don't ask because I'm not sure I really want to know. It doesn't really matter. "How long?"

"Shouldn't be too long." He pulls his hat down over his eyes and slouches down against the rock we've been sitting on.

I want to grill him more on Yedys, but he saved my life and Ben's so I give him space and quiet and head back to the truck instead. Manganaro is there putting the finishing touches on Ben's head bandage. I frown at Manganaro. "You could've told me Casilla was in the cab of the truck."

He doesn't look at me. "Where's the fun in that?"

Ignoring the joy punching him in the face would give me, I turn to Ben. "How's your head?"

"I'll live."

Thank god. "Good to hear."

"Sorry I wasn't much help getting out of there. I've just never gotten blown up before."

"Me neither."

Ben nods then winces and presses the middle three fingers of his right hand against his forehead. "I've never been shot at, either."

Manganaro climbs back into the truck to put the unused medical supplies away. When the flap falls shut, I kiss Ben. On his lips are salt, blood, and dust. My throat constricts and I have to pull away to catch my breath. I can't look at him. He gently touches my face with filthy fingers and turns my head to him.

"I'm okay."

"Only because you slipped. We got lucky, Ben. Really,

fucking lucky."

"Hey, we knew this would be risky. Maybe we didn't fully appreciate the possibility of getting blown up"—he tries to smile, but it doesn't fit his face, so he lets it drop—"but we knew there'd be risk. We accepted that. Both of us."

I nod, but I can't hold the gaze of his deep brown eyes too long. I stare off into the fading sun, wondering if Lincoln can see the sun right now or if he's alone in some stifling, tiny, dark cell. I shiver. No. Even if he's in a cell, it's better than the alternative.

Suddenly, I can't wait around doing nothing any longer. I turn my back to Ben and swallow hard.

"Did Casilla save your equipment?"

"What?"

I turn my head back to look at him. "The WHISP-boosting equipment, do we still have it?"

Ben stops halfway through shaking his head. "I don't know. Love, do you really think this is the time to...." He motions around at the barren landscape around us. "We could move out any minute, and I'd have to hook up the equipment to the truck's battery. Why don't we wait until we get to the new base camp?"

"Because I'm sick of waiting. I need to do something other than wait for us to get blown up or shot at again."

He gives me a hard look, but then relents. "Okay, okay. Just give me a minute to see if he even grabbed the equipment."

As he lifts the canvas and slowly raises himself into the truck, a hollow pit of guilt forms in my stomach. Yes, Ben is alive, but he's also in a lot of pain. I hadn't considered that he might really just want to lie down right now, that he might need to rest. But then, I think of Lincoln again and can't shake the feeling that we're running out of time. We can both rest when this is over, when we find Lincoln. I pick up the flap and follow Ben into the back of the truck.

CHAPTER 16

Excerpt Press Conference with Chief of Police Christopher Lowman
September 18th, 2026
…and I want the citizens of New York City to remember that these tragedies were caused not by a WHISP, but by a murderer named Rachel Chester and other disturbed humans, and that criminals, not WHISPs, are the real threat to our safety and security. Nevertheless, the City and State of New York have heard the growing concerns of our citizens and proposed a WHISP Task Force to face the challenges of cases involving WHISPs. It is my honor to announce that they have appointed me the position of head of this task force.

Liv, are you there? I don't hear any voices in my head, but there's maybe a tingle in the center of my back. *Is she mad at me for ignoring her?* Well, I'm mad at her for possibly getting us blown up. *Stop it. Not helping.* I take a deep breath and try to reach out with my senses instead of words, struggling to picture her shape behind me.

"Are you ready?"

I open my eyes and nod to Ben, though I don't particularly feel connected to Liv right now. We're a short way from the truck with Ben's equipment propped up on a rock facing me. My back, and Liv, are to the northeast, roughly in the direction of Yedys, according to Hardja. The idea today is that if Lincoln is there, I'll send out Liv to find him. It all seems a bit ludicrous since the prison camp is over a hundred miles away, but Chester sent Ray out at least thirty miles from Rikers, so theoretically, it's possible. Unless it was more of Ray leaving on her own and driving Chester insane, but I try not to think of that. "Sure."

The tendons on Ben's neck are protruding and, in the lantern light, creating bizarre shadows along his throat. He's worried and his anxiety isn't completely unfounded. The last time he did something like this to try to cure the WHISP virus, he almost killed me. "I'm starting out with a way lower frequency. It should cut back on the reverberation and any feedback from—"

"Babe. Just do it."

His Adam's apple bobs up and down. "Okay. But tell me if you feel anything at all. I'm serious, Sylvia. Don't wait until it hurts."

I nod.

He's unconvinced, but checks the dials for the twentieth time and flips a switch anyway. Nothing happens. Well, not nothing. A green light illuminates on one of the panels, the electronics start humming quietly, and Ben's face contorts in fear, but nothing happens to me. I let out a breath I didn't know I was holding. "I've got nothing. I think we need to bump it up."

"Just give it a little time. It may build up a resonance within the WHISP particles like vibrations in a bridge. Um, and maybe you should try to concentrate."

Annoyance ripples through me, but I close my eyes. *Go on,*

Liv, go find Lincoln. Who's a good WHISP? Nothing. Come on, focus. Your son's fucking life is at stake. But I can't honestly bring myself to believe that this, and not breaking down a door and shooting people, is going to help us save him. It's the same as with the virus. Liv helped with that, she can help with this. But somehow, it's not the same. *Please, Liv?* A phantom hand pats my belly and I jump, spinning around and bringing my fists up into a fighting stance. Of course, there's no one behind me.

"Syvly?" Ben's at my side. "Are you okay? What happened?"

I open my mouth to tell him that I think Liv is mad at me for putting my unborn child at risk, but then close it again. Taking a deep breath to slow my respiration and heartrate, I just shake my head. "It's nothing. I felt something. It was probably a bug. It just startled me. Sorry." In the poor light, I can't tell if he believes me or not, but my lies are saved from further scrutiny by Casilla.

"Pack up your stuff, we're moving out ASAP."

———

OUR NEW BASE OF OPERATIONS IS ON THE OUTSKIRTS of a town, though "town" might not be an appropriate description. It's a shamble of buildings around a central point. Our building is about the length of a football field away and sports its own goat pen complete with goats. We arrive in the dead of night, but the moon is still high and Casilla takes extra care this time to squirrel me away into the building before I'm spotted by any locals. By the light of a lantern, the inside looks about the same as our first hidey-hole with a threadbare couch, small kitchen area, and a small table with three chairs. The only thing missing is the desk with the electronics. I'm about to flop down on the couch when Casilla shakes his head and moves the couch a few feet to reveal a trapdoor. Of course, silly me thinking we'd be above ground for once. I can't help myself. "Really?"

Casilla shrugs. "It's actually better down there."

I find that hard to believe, but don't say so as I descend a ladder into darkness. About six feet under, my feet feel dirt. "Is it supposed to be pitch black?"

Above me, Casilla's lantern illuminates only a small patch around the ladder, and my fight or flight responds to the darkness around me as I back into the ladder wall and try to will my eyes to adjust.

"I'll rev up the generator, just give me a minute." He clatters down the ladder and strides toward the other side of the room like someone confident that nothing and no one is waiting for him in the dark.

I'm tempted to follow him for closeness sake, but then again, the ladder is the only way out of this pit, so I don't move. Instead, I watch his cone of light move to the other side of the room and illuminate a wall of electronics. He squats and fiddles with a black box on the ground, producing several sparks.

"Shit!"

Ozone fills my nostrils, and maybe a hint of burnt hair. Another light appears at the top of the ladder and Ben peers down at me.

"What's going on down there?"

"Casilla's trying to get the generator started."

There's more cursing from the far side of the room as Ben climbs down, dislodging dirt into my hair as the ladder shakes. When he reaches the bottom, he turns to me. "You okay?"

Nodding, I manage half a sad grin. "Yeah, but I'm afraid Casilla is going to electrocute himself." I say the last a bit louder than strictly necessary.

Ben glances across to Casilla. "Can I give you a hand?"

The light is too poor to make out his expression, but Casilla's voice is clear with annoyance. "Sure! Have at it!"

The men pass each other and Casilla grumbles about finding another generator as he climbs the ladder. Though Casilla would've been much better protection from an ambush, my body relaxes with Ben here and I stumble across the room to him.

"Can I help?"

Ben returns my sad half-grin. "Sure. Hold up the lantern for me."

Crouching, I pick up the light and hold it over the slightly smoking generator. The bright white light from the LEDs is almost blinding up close after standing in the gloom. I tilt it away from me and blink furiously to dissipate the spots, then watch Ben methodically check wires and use his shirt to clean dust and grime from connections. Despite being a physicist nerd, he's good with his hands. Lincoln, too, who didn't inherit the skill from me. My heart arrests painfully in my chest then starts up again. I find Ben staring at me.

"What's wrong?"

I shake my head. "Nothing. I was just thinking about"—the pain in my chest returns—"Lincoln." It's almost sacrilege to say his name aloud. "You... He's a lot like you."

Ben's head bobs up and down. "You remind me of him, too, sometimes."

"Yeah? Like when?"

Returning his gaze to the generator, he sniffs. "Like when he's being stubborn for no reason, like the time we took him to Central Park and he insisted we feed the swans because everyone else was feeding the ducks."

"I remember."

"And when—"

I touch his arm gently. "Don't. It sounds like we're giving a eulogy."

Ben swallows hard, but doesn't reply. We let the silence linger, though it's broken now and then by voices from above. My legs are protesting, but getting more comfortable or sitting seems like giving up on Ben's ability to fix the generator, so I try to keep the light still even when my legs start shaking. I can't give up. We can't give up.

"There."

Ben flicks a switch and the generator coughs to life, bringing with it a pale glow from a half dozen overhead bulbs. The room is larger than I thought it was, at least twice as big as the bunker in Bez Imeni. But that being said, it's only one room with bunks pushed up against three walls in one half, and no bathroom in sight. Never thought I'd miss the bucket. Standing, I turn off the lantern and squeeze Ben's arm.

"Holy shit, you did it." Halfway down the ladder with a heavy duffle on his back, Casilla can't hide his surprise.

I squeeze Ben's arm again.

CHAPTER 17

Journal Excerpt Dr. Ahmed Mahadow
Tuesday, November 27th, 2029
RNA Vector Test: 5:00 p.m. EST
Preliminary results indicate a significant change in the
wave impulses of subject 477's WHISP. Though this
specific vector also has caused electrochemical disrup-
tions in greater primates and humans without WHISPs,
Dr. Higgins's research suggests a modified vector might
only affect those with WHISPs. Further genetic testing is
needed.

BEN HAS THE WHISP AMPLIFIER SET UP AGAIN. I'M
trying to explain to him that it won't work because Liv is mad
at me for endangering the baby, but he won't listen and tells
me I'm just not focused enough. I'm also worried because the
amplifier is smoking and sparking, but Ben doesn't seem to
notice.

"Ready?"

"No, wait!"

He flips the switch and my whole body starts to vibrate.
Buzz, buzz, buzz. My skin is breaking along unseen seams,

cracks running down my arms to my fingernails. Buzz, buzz, buzz. The cracks become finer and finer until they are splitting my molecules apart. Buzz, buzz, buzz. I lift my hand, but see only a gray shadow hand where my flesh used to be. I turn my head and Liv stares back at me with cool hazel eyes. Buzz, buzz, buzz.

My cell phone vibrates against my hip in the pocket of my fatigues. Opening my eyes, I stare up at the wooden planks of the bunk above me. I wonder if Ben is getting any sleep. I'm surprised myself that I dozed off, considering the number of people in the room, but it's quiet as a funeral, other than the annoying buzz from my phone and the murmur of hushed voices. The phone buzzes again. *All right, Crone, give me a second.* Shifting so I can access my pocket, I pull the phone out and turn on the screen.

Crone: 911

Harbinger: What's wrong?

Crone: 10-0, Code 2, 11-58

Caution. Urgent, don't use a siren or flash cruiser lights. Police radios being monitored, use your cell. *What the hell?* I bite my lip. Why would Crone be using police codes with me? Unless...Caution. Don't let anyone know something's up. Are you being monitored? 10-4 is too obvious a reply.

Harbinger: 10-36

This information is confidential.

I sit up further and pull the thin blanket so that it acts as a shield between my legs, but glancing around the room, no one is paying attention to me. Casilla is napping in another bunkbed, Hardja is manning the electronics and surveillance, I think Manganaro is keeping watch in the house above, and the rest of the team are playing cards.

Crone: Who are you with?

I consider the ramifications of telling him the truth. If Casilla found out I'd outed the CIA's involvement he could...

what? Send me home? Have me arrested? Shoot me? Refuse to rescue Lincoln? Plus, it wasn't like I was telling the press. Crone wouldn't tell anyone. Also, I could erase these texts, couldn't I?

Harbinger: CIA

Crone: Thought so.

Harbinger: Why?

Crone: Things have gone to shit. Bodies of virus victims missing (clerical error!) HS working with FBI to get survivors in witness protection, but WHISPs make it hard. In safe house now, but HS is twitchy as fuck.

Harbinger: Okay. But why the cloak and dagger? You said HS thought this was part of something bigger right?

Crone: Rumor going around CIA involved.

Okay. It would make total sense for other agencies to assume the CIA would handle things outside of the U.S. I'm missing something.

Harbinger: Involved in what?

Crone: In the virus.

The phone starts to slip from my numb hands. I reposition it as my eyes dart around the room again. *Don't look freaked out, Sylvy, try to look bored; no, annoyed.* I dip my head, ease the piano-wire tension from my shoulders, and then puff my cheeks and let out a sighing breath. My rushing blood and thumping heart refuse to slow. Maybe I'm misunderstanding Crone.

Harbinger: How?

Crone: As in they made it with the Rubezi terrorists.

Harbinger: Why?

Crone: Think Harbinger! They do spy shit, right? What if everyone could do stuff they train years for with WHISPs? What if WHISPs infiltrate the Pentagon? How would you fight an army of WHISPs? WHISPs freaky for us, but must be threatening for CIA. Military. Government. WHISPs like Chester's must make them shit themselves.

Harbinger: Why not just recruit?

Crone: Could, but WHISP double agent? Even scarier. Easier to just eliminate threat, right?

Harbinger: But why would Rubezi want to kill 44% of their people?

Crone: ? Some sort of ethnic cleansing?

Could be, I guess. Casilla said most of the population with WHISPs were poor, maybe they were also rebellious? Another possibility is that it would make their leader look like a god if he could rid the country of WHISPs. But still, forty-four percent of the population is a lot to lose. Wouldn't it be better to recruit those WHISPers into a WHISP army rather than murder them all? If properly trained, there's no telling what all those WHISPs could be capable of in terms of espionage or assassination. A chill runs through my blood. How could the Rubezi government throw away such a valuable cache of resources? And why were they testing the virus in the U.S. when there were so many more test subjects in Rubezikan?

Crone: Thought you'd be a little more concerned with CIA involvement.

I look around the room again. *Was Hardja just turning away from me?*

Harbinger: Point. But sounds a little conspiracy theory. Any proof?

Crone: Working on it. Be careful.

Harbinger: I will. You too.

Waiting for a full minute before I'm sure Crone has no more to say, I then delete the text thread up to the 911. I have to tell Ben. Or do I? What if Crone's got it wrong? What if the rumors are just conspiracy theory bullshit? I'd worry him for no reason. And if it is true that the CIA's involved in the creation of the virus somehow, Ben doesn't have the best poker face. If they suspected that we knew something, they might kill us. But wait. Why haven't they killed us already? No one but Crone knows where we are. They could've shot Ben and I and left us in the desert. Why even bring us to Rubezikan to begin with unless.... It's because I told them I could cure the virus and they want to study how I did it? And Ben? Because he was researching the virus? Then why not just kidnap us and take us directly to the lab in Yedys? Why make all this pretense of a mission to save Lincoln?

No, there's something I'm missing, and I can't tell Ben anything until I'm sure of what's going on. But how can I figure out what's going on? *Hey Casilla, just wondering, are you really in cahoots with the Rubezi terrorists?* No. But maybe.... *Liv? I know you're mad, but we're all in this together now and you know I'm not leaving without Lincoln, so I need your help.*

There's an itch between my shoulder blades that I take as a good sign.

I know no one else here has a WHISP, but can you like read their auras? Get a feel for their electromagnetic fields? Just an impression? Leaning back, I close my eyes and force my muscles to unclench. I am open, reaching out, sending Liv out.

Above me, Ben shifts in his bunk and the boards creak. A sense of peace washes over me. Then abruptly the peace is replaced by a sense of being stretched taut and thin. Under this is a vibration of calm, but one far different than the peacefulness. A moment later the discomfort of the stretching turns painful and briefly there's an undercurrent of turmoil, but then it's replaced by a swell of nausea. My eyes fly open and I sit up. Breathing through my mouth, I hold back the vomit while searching for a place to puke should I be unsuccessful. There's no garbage can, and the pit toilet is up the ladder just off the main structure, so the sink is the only option.

"Hey, you okay?" One of the agents at the table, Onai, has finally noticed me. "Are you gonna throw up?"

The other agents are all looking at me now with varying degrees of annoyance and disgust on their faces.

Hardja doesn't look away from the surveillance equipment, but chimes in, "Someone get her a bucket."

I want to tell them I'm fine and to go fuck themselves but doing so would be dangerous right now.

"Sylvy?"

Oh great. Ben's awake now.

Concern replacing drowsiness, he leans over the side of his bunk. "Are you okay?"

There's a round of snickering from the other side of the room. Cop pride and my own mule-stubborn disposition kicks in. I am not going to give them the satisfaction....

Shit! I run for the sink and make it just in time. A ghostly hand rubs my back as I empty my stomach into the grungy plastic basin.

CHAPTER 18

After reports of certain WHISP anomalies, members of
the UN have passed a resolution that condemns using
WHISPs in any kind of international espionage or
warfare and classifies such an action as a war crime. For
more information, and to view the agreement, please go
to UN.org/WHISPstreatise. ~ CNN.com

THANKFULLY, MOST OF THE AGENTS THINK I'M
experiencing traveler's belly, though Casilla's throwing me
wary looks. Ben holds out a MRE macaroni and cheese.

"Do you think you can eat this one?"

I take it from him but don't look him in the eye. "I'm fine
now." Not entirely true, but I think I can keep myself from
barfing again. It was just stress from Crone's texts combined
with me trying to push Liv's tether...and the fact that I'm pregnant. *Did they say how far along? No, of course not, how could they
know without an ultrasound?*

"Sylvy?"

I've been holding the green packet without opening it for
too long. "Hmmm?"

"Are you sure you're okay?" Ben's dropped his voice to a whisper.

I meet his gaze. "I won't be okay until we get Lincoln back."

"You know what I mean."

I tear open the packet and retrieve a plastic spork from a pouch on the side that also contains a ketchup packet. *Yuck.* I sigh. "I probably won't upchuck again unless I put ketchup on the macaroni and cheese." I hold up the little packet.

Ben's wince is what I assume is an attempt at a grin. He takes a bite of his own MRE and the wince turns into a full grimace. He swallows the bite with difficulty. "Or unless you have some of mine." He checks the label again and shakes his head. "Our poor men in uniform."

"Hey, what about us poor CIA agents?" Casilla sits beside Ben at the table with his own MRE, chicken and dumplings.

I suppress a gag. "From T.V. and various movies, I'm given to understand you agents often get to eat at very expensive restaurants while you pretend to be diplomats and such."

"Damn media. I haven't eaten at a restaurant in probably a month. McDonald's doesn't count."

Trying to appear at ease, I take a small bite from my MRE. It tastes surprisingly like Play-Doh and I have nothing but slightly gritty, warm water to wash it down with, so the taste lingers. The ketchup may not be so bad a plan after all.

"Do you ever get used to these?" Ben holds up his MRE, beef stew.

Casilla shakes his head. "No, but sometimes we smuggle the ones backpackers use on a mission. Those are so much better." He flutters his eyelids a bit. "These, however, don't have an expiration date."

I can't keep up the small talk anymore. "So, what are we waiting for now?"

He sighs and sets down his chicken and dumplings analogue.

"There's supposed to be another shipment to Yedys in eight hours. The plan is to stake out the shipment, find out where the supplies are going, follow them into the lab, and make the extraction."

"Are we going to blow up the lab when we leave?" Ben's voice is strained.

I stare at him.

He swallows hard. "It's an honest question. It's a terrorist lab at a prison camp."

His face a mask, Casilla only hesitates a moment before answering, "It's not our primary goal."

"That's not a no," I point out.

Ben's face suddenly pales. "What about the other prisoners?"

"What about them?" Casilla's voice is bland.

"If we blow up the lab, couldn't the other prisoners be killed?"

"Very likely so."

Realization dawns on Ben, whose face takes on a kicked puppy expression. "Oh. I don't suppose it's possible for us to free everyone then?"

"And make it out alive?" Casilla shakes his head. "Probably not."

I can almost see Ben's internal monologue. 'Do you want to leave a terrorist lab up and running?' 'But what about all those innocent people?' 'They were probably going to be executed anyway. We would definitely be saving more people than we killed.' 'But—'

"Hey." Casilla puts his hand on Ben's shoulder and leans in. "Don't tear yourself up about it. It's not your decision. It's not even mine. It's out of our hands." He leans back and removes his hand. "Just worry about your son."

Ben gives a shaky nod. "I take it you do this a lot, then. Follow orders that get people killed."

Casilla's face turns hard. "People get killed every day. I try to ensure it's mostly bad people."

"I wasn't…. I mean, is that how you deal with it? Fall back on the greater good?"

I watch Casilla. Is he the kind of man who would think that creating a virus to kill all people with WHISPs is part of the greater good? I don't think he is.

"Not that I have to justify myself to you, Doc, but everyone has to believe in something. I decided to believe in my country, in democracy. Morality is all fine and good until somebody has to make a hard decision. I decided to let others make the hard decisions for me and have faith in them. You should have more faith in them, too. They sent us to rescue your son, after all."

I don't know if Casilla's speech makes me like him more or less. I've had to follow orders before that let scumbags back on the street because of lost evidence or scared witnesses or because the DA didn't want to waste the city's money on a case she didn't think we could win. I suppose I've let others make the hard decisions for me, too. But Casilla probably wouldn't have thrown in that last part about rescuing Lincoln if he was planning on killing him or forcefully recruiting us all to a WHISP virus project. My cop instincts aren't telling me he's lying, but then again, he's probably better trained to lie than anyone I've ever dealt with before.

Ben clears his throat. "So, what's my part going to be? Am I going to stay in the truck and run surveillance? 'Cause I think I can run most of your equipment, but I'd like to make sure I know what I'm doing."

A hint of surprise registers on Casilla's face. "I thought you'd want to be there breaking down the door."

"That's her job." Ben points at me. "Getting blown up and shot at and being useless has given me a new perspective."

Casilla nods. "Good. After dinner, Manganaro can give you a

rundown. All you should really have to do is push the panic button if you see reinforcements coming."

Ben stands with his barely touched MRE in hand. "I'm ready."

Casilla's mouth opens, then shuts and he tilts his head toward Manganaro at the surveillance desk.

Ben's shoulders straighten with purpose as he heads over. Good. I was worried about Ben being on the ground, too. I've taken him shooting before and he, at least, knows how to release a safety, but he has no natural talent with firearms.

I lean closer to Casilla. "Just so you know, if there are other captives being held with Lincoln, I'm not leaving them behind."

He nods slightly and his eyes find mine. "You could get us all killed that way."

I stare him down. "Lincoln would never forgive me and I'd never forgive myself."

"If we all die because of you, you won't have the luxury of guilt."

"True."

"You know, I could force you to stay in the truck with your husband. Why would you tell me that?"

I shrug. "Because I didn't think you'd feel good about leaving people behind, either, and so we're on the same page in there."

"Somebody always gets left behind or caught in the crossfire."

I nod. "Doesn't mean we shouldn't try."

"Look, Harbinger, when I say we need to get out, we need to get out, all right? I'm not sacrificing my agents for random strangers."

Anger flares, hot and close to my heart. "Then why do this mission, at all? Lincoln means the world to me, but if he's just a stranger to you, then why bother to save him?"

Casilla doesn't flinch. "It's the mission."

"Is it?" I search his face. "You said blowing up the lab wasn't the primary mission, but you didn't say saving Lincoln was the primary goal, either. What is the primary goal?"

"Sorry. You're on a need-to-know basis, and you don't need to know."

"Like Hell. I'm risking my life, Ben's risking his, we need to know."

"Your mission is your son. I'd worry more about that."

An ache in my jaw tells me I'm grinding my teeth, but antagonizing Casilla isn't helping Lincoln. If the CIA is there for some more sinister reason, Casilla isn't going to tell me, and probably I'm better off not knowing. Still, I take a calming breath and try one more time. "I do get where you're coming from, but there's a chance I could fuck up the primary goal if I don't know what it is."

Casilla gives me a long look. "No, there isn't."

CHAPTER 19

Recovered File CAW Server
Date: May 10, 2025
Subject: 8841 (Poppy)
Test: WHISP Generation
Since no signs of a WHISP have manifested, further
exposure to high levels of electromagnetic radiation on
this chimp seems cruel at best given the cancer lesions
in the animal's skin, lymph nodes, brain, and lungs. At
this stage, euthanasia is strongly recommended.

On Casilla's gentle prodding of usefulness,
Ben and I are in the building above the new bunker trying the
amplifier again, and I'm trying to figure out what the primary
objective of the CIA's mission is. It's possible that blowing up
the laboratory is the primary goal and Casilla was just lying. If
the CIA is working with the terrorists then the primary goal
could be to deliver us to the laboratory, but then why not just
go straight there? Maybe some other party is trying to stop the
CIA from getting to the lab? No, that makes no sense. Maybe
the CIA was working with the terrorists, or at least pretending
to, but then the terrorists released the virus and the CIA is

trying to cut ties with them? Or, the CIA created the WHISP virus and the terrorists stole it from them and the primary goal of the mission is to get the virus back. *Oh shit.* That actually makes sense. Or does it? I massage my temples, but the throb in my brain doesn't abate.

"Sylvy?" Ben's staring at me. "We don't have to do this now. If you're feeling sick...."

"No, I'm fine. Let's go."

He sighs, but nods. "Okay, because you didn't feel anything last time, I'm going to bump up the frequency, just a little. Tell me right away if anything feels off."

"Is safe for me to be here with that thing? I won't get a WHISP from it, dah?" Agent Valcross glances up from his position at one of the windows.

Ben frowns. "I've been working with equipment like this for about a year now and no one in our laboratory has developed a WHISP—"

Here it comes. Ben's not only a terrible liar, but he's terrible at lying.

"—but there's usually more shielding."

Muttering in another language, Valcross scowls and shifts his chair a useless few inches away from us before resuming his watch out the window. After playing several light-hearted rounds of gin rummy with Valcross earlier, I'm not sure whether the annoyance in his face is real or affected for comedic purposes.

Ben clears his throat and nods to me.

I return the nod and close my eyes. The hum of the machine tells me Ben's turned it on. This time, I do think I feel a vibration in my chest. *Can you feel it too, Liv? Go. Find my son.* I try to push her away from me, but the stretching sensation quickly turns to pain. Without meaning to, I gasp. The vibrations and pain stop and I open my eyes. Ben's in front of me.

"What happened?"

I don't feel like lying to him anymore. "It started to hurt."

Dejected, he nods.

I touch his hand. "But I do think I felt it working. It's just...."

"Just what?"

I lower my voice. "I think Liv is kinda attached to me right now."

He doesn't get it. "I'm not sure what you mean. Isn't she always attached?"

"I mean, right now, especially." I move his hand to graze my stomach.

He looks down at his hand. "Oh." He looks back at me. "Ohhh." Ben glances at Valcross but he's not looking at us. Ben touches my belly gently with the back of his finger then brings my hand up and kisses it. "I have to say. The possibility of that affecting things hadn't crossed my mind."

"Mine either, really, but it's either that or she's just not like...can't do that." I'd been about to say Liv wasn't like Chester's WHISP, Ray, but I couldn't. The memory of Chester in her room at Kirby invades my mind. "Or maybe I'm just afraid."

Ben squeezes my hand. "Afraid of Liv?"

"What? No. Afraid that if she left me and something happened to her...."

"Oh." He looks away. "I, uh, I didn't really think of that, either."

"That's because you didn't see *her*."

He turns back and nods then hugs me. "I'm sorry. We'll stop."

"But if this could help Lincoln...." My eyes burn with the seeds of tears.

He pulls back to look at me. "If something happened to her, it wouldn't help Lincoln *and* it would hurt you. It isn't necessary. We know where he is and it's not like Liv could bring him back with her, right?"

I raise an eyebrow. "Of course not, but she might be able to see door codes or back entrances, tell us exactly where Lincoln is in the compound, stuff like that."

Ben's eyes dart to Valcross, then to the couch, then back to me. "I don't think Casilla is the type to storm into an enemy compound without knowing at least a little about what to expect. And it's not like these guys haven't done this before."

"Maybe I've lost a little faith in them since we got blown up." Or maybe I've lost faith in them since Crone told me they might be working with the terrorists. As I stare into Ben's eyes, the desire to tell him what Crone said is so strong I nearly open my mouth. But I don't. I want him to share this burden with me and be able to confide in him, but it's selfish. If it's all true, I don't know how Ben knowing will help matters, and if Crone's got his wires crossed, it'll freak Ben out for no reason.

"Let's pretend getting blown up was a fluke. I mean, look, we haven't gotten—"

"Don't say it!" caution tinges Valcross's tone. "Is bad luck." He turns back to the window and I have to wonder how much of our conversation he heard.

Suddenly, I'm glad I didn't try to confide in Ben. In fact, it was pretty stupid of me to even whisper anything about the baby. The whole building could be wired for sound as well as video surveillance. *Is Casilla watching us right now?* Invisible spiders skitter up and down my legs and back as I feel unseen eyes on me. Will trying to act normal now fix anything? Maybe. Couldn't hurt.

"Guess I'm just not a super WHISPer."

"Nah, you're just plain super." Ben kisses my hand again. "And we're going to get out of this, all of us, together."

I wish I had his optimism. My hip buzzes. I'm torn. If Crone has more information for me, I need to know. At the same time, I can't exactly hide my text conversation from Ben without it being weird.

At that moment, Ben saves me. "Sorry, I'll be right back." He makes his way to a short walkway that connects the main structure of the house to the outhouse.

When the outhouse door closes behind him, I casually pull out my phone. Pretending the sunlight is obscuring the screen, I tilt it back and forth and then shield it with my hand before reading Crone's text.

Crone: Just checking in.

Harbinger: Any updates?

Crone: No. Still haven't found virus bodies.

Harbinger: Any confirmations on what you told me before?

Crone: No sorry.

I grit my teeth. It's nice that Crone wants to make sure I'm still alive, but I expected more intel. Then I get an idea. Jeffrey would never talk about something like a CIA conspiracy over the phone, but he might talk to Crone about it in person. Then again, he was the one who put me in contact with Casilla in the first place. But maybe he didn't know about the CIA's involvement until after he gave me Casilla's number and didn't want to endanger me by trying to warn me. Oh God, do I hate this. Can I trust anyone? Yes. I can trust Crone and I can trust Jeffrey. And Ben, of course. I glance up at the door on the far side of the room. Time's wasting.

Harbinger: See if you can confirm anything with Jeffrey Kearn at the FBI. He's the one who did Chester's copycat profile for us. Old friend. Tell him you've been in contact with me.

Crone: Okay. Anything else?

The door opens.

Harbinger: No. Let me know what he says.

As soon as I hit send, I delete the thread and turn off my

phone just as Ben reaches me and pulls a small bottle of hand sanitizer from his pocket.

He douses his hands liberally and rubs them together. "Crone?"

Nodding, I pocket the cell. "Who else?"

"Any leads on their end? There haven't been any other incidents have there?"

"No, nothing like that. Well except…" I watch Valcross in my peripheral vision.

"Except what?"

"Except the bodies of the WHISP virus victims have gone missing."

Valcross shows no reaction to the news. Ben, on the other hand….

"What! What the fuck? What do you mean they went missing?"

I shrug. "Apparently there was some clerical error and they got moved, but no one seems to know where."

Again, Valcross doesn't give an indication that he's listening. Maybe he's too nonchalant about it? Suspicion stirs in my chest until he finally stands and stretches.

"Fucking bureaucrats. Would accidentally deport own mother messing up paperwork." He points to the amplifier. "You are done for now?"

I glance at Ben's taut face, then nod.

Valcross's mouth spreads into a wide, slightly sinister grin. "Good. Time for rematch."

CHAPTER 20

"The theory of overexposure to things like cell phones and computers doesn't hold up to the reality of WHISP conversion in more remote and less technologically advanced cultures."

"You have a different theory, Dr. Lightfall?"

"Yes, I do. I think that it is less a matter of amount of exposure and more a matter of the type of technology one is exposed to. Epidemiological models suggest the introduction of a specific wave-emitting or wave-modifying piece of technology a few years before the WHISP phenomenon that spread rapidly throughout the world in many different electronic devices, not just cell phones and computers."

"Is there any hint of what piece of technology we're talking about? Could my new smart fridge have the potential to give me a WHISP?"

"Unfortunately, it could be something as small as the etchings on a microchip, and it's very difficult to trace the small advances that happen with technology every day all over the world, so I'd have to say it's a possibility."

~ Dateline Interview Dr. Jorden Lightfall, CDC Epidemiologist

CASILLA ZOOMS IN ON THE SATELLITE IMAGE UNTIL the compound comes into view. The rectangular walls surround four clusters of buildings of various sizes. The only road passes through what must be a gate in one narrow wall and ends at a large building in the center of the walled area. All I can think is that the place looks like a fortified labyrinth. Lincoln could be in or under any one of those buildings. Casilla taps one of the structures and it enlarges.

"We have good intel that this is where most of the shipments that bypass the guards are going, so it's a good bet this is where the lab is. Here's what we have as far as schematics for that building." Casilla brings up a photo on one of the other screens.

The schematics are a crude sketch on a piece of paper.

"That's all we've got?" It isn't easy to keep the disappointment out of my voice.

He nods. "We're lucky to have this. It's second hand from a former guard, but should be accurate enough to get us in the facility. And it's not like the Rubezi government has to file building plans with the city's building commission. If there is an actual blueprint for Yedys, which I seriously doubt, it's tucked away in a file cabinet in one of the marble wonders in the capital city, Tarbygan, where even the CIA can't get to it."

There's a shared chuckle from the agents around the table, but Casilla doesn't join in or smile.

"Surveillance says most of the shipments are left at a loading door here." He points to a door at one end of the building. "If the lab is underground, the access point would be close to that outer door. No sense in hauling heavy equipment any farther than they have to. After we're inside the wall, we'll enter there. Shouldn't be a guard outside the door, but we're not sure about inside. There's an electronic lock on the door, so Valcross will take point with that."

I see a large flaw in their plan. "Wait. Back up a second. This is all inside this wall which I'm guessing is like fifteen feet tall, topped with razor wire, lit up like a Christmas tree at night, and lined with machinegun-toting guards. How will we get anywhere near the wall, let alone inside of it to this building?"

"This is where we're going to get a little help. I've arranged two rather large distractions, one of which is a missile strike to the main generator which will have the power out for ten to fifteen minutes. That's our window. According to our sources, there's a good place to get over the wall here next to the water tower." He zooms out the satellite image and points to a section of the wall with an adjacent round, white shape.

This sounds like a terrible plan. "Okay, what about getting out again? I'm guessing the whole place will be on alert after a missile strike to the main generator."

"No. The whole place will be on alert and focused here and here because of the frontal assault that will take place shortly after, which is the second distraction."

My frown deepens. "Assault?" I know that these people have my son, that they're probably experimenting on him right now, that they tried to release a WHISP virus that could've killed thousands, if not millions, of people, that the assault Casilla is talking about is on a prison camp in a virtual despotism; still, it sounds like a lot of people getting killed. "Won't that endanger the prisoners, too?"

He gives me a do-you-want-your-son-back-or-not stare. "Hopefully not, since it won't target the main cellblock, but I have to break it to you, Yedys is not a place people normally come back from."

I don't agree with his justification that any unlucky prisoner was probably going to die anyway, but since the attacks aren't targeting the cellblock, I can't argue with him. Really, I couldn't argue with him anyway since I don't see any other way of getting in and out. Ben is quiet, but I see the same misgivings in his face. People will die so we can get Lincoln back.

I swallow hard. "Who's running the attack? Another CIA team?"

"No."

I wait, but Casilla doesn't continue. He isn't going to tell us who. It's probably best I don't know, anyway. Less guilt if they're strangers, if I never learn how many casualties occur.

"Any more questions, Detective, or can we get back to the plan?"

My silence fills the room. Casilla nods and turns his attention back to the hand drawing. "My guess is that the entrance is this inner door here, and intel says this one is also an electronic lock, so it'll be Valcross again unless he's down, then it'll be Hardja."

That comment brings another question to my lips, one I can't keep quiet about. "How many casualties until we abort?"

Hardja snorts, but a look from Casilla quiets him.

"There is no abort protocol for a mission like this," Casilla's voice is hard.

Ben finally says, "But you said I was going to monitor the situation and let you know if something went wrong so you could get out."

"I never said that."

"Then what's the fucking point of my surveillance?"

Wow, Ben is really pissed.

Casilla frowns. "The point, is so that you can relay to us what each person's situation is if we get separated and to let us know if the extraction point is clear."

"No, that's bullshit, you'll have earpieces, you don't need me monitoring, I'm coming in, too."

"No, you're not!" Casilla stands and has Ben against the wall slightly faster than I have my gun to his head, which is a hair quicker than Hardja has his gun to my head.

"Take your hands off my husband."

Although stunned silent by Casilla's violence, Ben is quick to recover. "What are you going to do, shoot me?"

"No." Casilla doesn't even look at me. "But I will tie you up and put you in a safe place until this is all over, Doctor."

"No, you won't." I hold steady even as Hardja presses his barrel into my skull.

Casilla releases Ben, who falls to the floor, and finally turns to me so that my gun barrel is between his eyes. "Is that right?"

Ben spins away and gets to his feet with raised fists, but Onai and Manganaro are on him and grab his arms before he can take a swing at Casilla.

Casilla could probably take my gun away from me before I shot him, but only because I'm distracted by Hardja's gun leaving a bruise on my occipital bone. I lower my gun from Casilla's face, but only because he let go of Ben. "I'll be responsible for him."

Casilla suddenly looks about ten years older. Older and tired. He signals to Hardja with his head and Hardja takes his gun away from my scalp. Then Casilla turns to Onai and Manganaro and sweeps out his hand palm down. As they release Ben, I catch his eye and shake my head once. Casilla faces me again and sighs.

"That's not the issue. Really. We need someone on the outside coordinating and he's the obvious choice. Smart, but no combat training. I need you focused in there, not worrying about two members of your family getting killed." He turns back to Ben. "It isn't bullshit. I plan on making the extraction with your son and I need to make sure the way is going to be clear. I don't want to get out of there only to be ambushed five feet from the fucking truck. Also, yeah, we'll have audio, but I won't be able to see what Hardja is seeing. You will."

Anger draining from his cheeks and the fight leaving his shoulders, Ben's gaze wanders down to the gun in my hand then up to my face. I nod. He deflates. I want to tell him that we need him in the truck, but he won't hear that. He feels useless, especially now that the WHISP amplifier isn't working, and there's nothing I can say that will change how he feels right now. I've been there, recently, sitting in quarantine while terrorists were slipping through my fingers. It's a horrible feeling.

"Look. Let's all just take a minute, okay? We still have a few hours before we have to leave and there's not much more to the plan without lab schematics. Get in, get the kid, get out. Manganaro, Hardja, with me. I wanna check the truck and do a full perimeter sweep before we start loading up."

Casilla heads to the ladder and climbs. Manganaro and Hardja follow without looking at me or Ben. The rest of the agents, except Valcross, also avoid eye contact as they busy themselves or flop down on one of the bunks. Valcross gives Ben a manly pat on the back and winks at me before sitting down at the table and dealing himself a round of solitaire. I holster my gun, step up to Ben, and take his hand, but he spins away and heads over to where the amplifier equipment is gathered along the wall. Without a word, he begins disassembling it for transport. The trap door bangs shut and I glance up at it, wondering if Casilla is going over the real mission with Manganaro and Hardja. Or maybe he already went over it with the rest of the team while Ben and I were trying the amplifier again earlier. *But then shouldn't he have taken Valcross with him? Maybe Valcross doesn't know what's going on. No, that doesn't make any sense, he's too close with Casilla to be in the dark.*

Crossing back to the desk with the surveillance equipment,

I search for Casilla and the other two on the screen. After a moment, I spot them walking away from the house, but I can't see their faces.

Department of Homeland Security Internal Communication
Hana Siddiqui
Re: New York WHISP Task Force
I have found the NYPD-headed task force to be woefully inept in their handling of the bioterrorist attack on the WHISP shelter as well as in their handling of the laboratory raid. Though they coordinated with State Police, Homeland Security should have been notified and included in the raid. It is my recommendation that the WHISP Task Force be absorbed into the Homeland Security umbrella and a new head appointed from DHS ranks ASAP. While the enforcement and laboratory of the task force may remain with the NYPD, all administration should immediately be moved to the Homeland Security office on Varick Street.

As the sun drops below the horizon behind us, we head southeast into the coming night. Ben hasn't said much since Casilla manhandled him and now sits beside me staring at nothing. Crone never got back to me, and Casilla made us all dump our cellphones into a sack before heading out. I'm truly on my own now. Maybe it was all just rumors about the CIA being involved with the terrorists. I can't make it make sense any other way, and if they are involved, what can I really do about it? Right now, I need to focus on Lincoln, on getting him out. After that, we'll have to take things one step at a time.

———

WE DRIVE FOR ABOUT THREE HOURS THEN THE TRUCK grinds to a halt. This is where we go the rest of the way on foot. Casilla said it would be about five miles. I'm not looking forward to it even though I'll be carrying less than half the weight of the others. Manganaro rummages around in the first aid kit then hands me a small packet with two tablets in it.

"For nausea." He breathes and turns away.

Stunned, I'm not sure if he knows about the baby or just knows that I threw up again earlier or if these are sedatives in some greater plot. I pocket them as I check my gun and ammo clips. Valcross is setting up screens and giving Ben last minute instructions while Ben sits passively on a crate. I wait until Valcross leaves him then slide up next to Ben. He doesn't look at me.

"Hey. This is your wife going off to get shot at here. I'm used to a little more of a goodbye."

When he turns to me, Ben's empty face is terrifying. "What if I watch it all right here?"

"Watch what?"

"Watch you and Lincoln die?"

Then it really hits me, why Ben doesn't want to be left behind. I imagine myself sitting on that crate, unable to do anything but stare as bullets rip through Ben and Lincoln; seeing their deaths from Ben's perspective until the feed from his helmet camera goes dark; screaming at a video screen. If everything went to hell, I'd be all alone in that truck in the desert. Would I drive away? To where? Would I radio for help? Would help come before troops from Yedys found me? Or would I just lie down in the truck, waiting for whatever happened? What would Ben do?

Picturing him lying on his back in the truck with dead eyes is too much for me. I throw my arms around him and squeeze until I can't breathe. Ben has the hardest job of us all. I say the only thing I can say, "We're going to make it out. Believe in me. Believe in Lincoln. We're both fighters. And you'll guide us and protect us. You'll be our guardian angel watching over us." I pull back and hold his face in both my hands. "I promise you, we're coming back to you." *I'll do everything in my power to get back to you.*

We will do everything. Liv's presence is little more than a fading echo, but for just a moment, it's there, an inkling of untapped strength. It's as unsettling as it is reassuring, but I'll take any help right now. We will do everything.

Some life returns to Ben's face, bringing with it, resolve. He sniffs, then nods, then leans in and kisses me. Painfully sweet, it's not our last kiss, but if it was...

"Remember. You promised me. You promised me, Sylvy."

All my words have gone, dissolved in a promise, and sealed with a kiss. I nod.

———

THE HIKE THROUGH THE DESERT DOES NOTHING TO keep my mind occupied or my heart from aching. Despite the lingering heat of the day, the fear in my guts is colder than the black of the ocean's depths. It's not a fear of death. Not really. It's a fear of breaking my promise, of leaving Ben behind. But even underneath that, there's another pain, one I've been ignoring and denying until now in the dark and quiet, the calm before the storm. In coming here, dragging Ben in my wake, insisting on doing this myself, and taking the coward's way instead of letting the CIA rescue Lincoln without me, I've endangered not just three lives, but a life not yet begun. *What kind of person am I?* Pressed up against the void, I'm flooded with regret from choices that cannot be undone when Casilla raises a hand.

Ahead, the glow of Yedys is beautiful and horrible. It's a beacon, a fortress, maybe the last place I'll ever see. Insurmountable walls around a vast miniature city, and somewhere inside, my baby. My first baby. Whatever hope or confidence I may have felt vanishes. This is a place shored up against armies. How can we possibly think to infiltrate it, plumb its depths, and escape again with our lives? Foolishness. Insanity. The idle chatter of overconfident CIA pricks.

Casilla motions us forward again, but our pace is much closer to a crawl. Valcross and Hardja have their infrared goggles on and are continuously scanning around us. Manganaro is in front with a device meant to identify landmines buried up to three feet underground. We haven't encountered any yet, that we know of, but we're still about a half mile from the facility. I'm nauseated, but for once it's not due to the baby inside me.

About a football field away from the wall, just outside the perimeter of harsh white light, on Casilla's signal, we all drop to the ground. How long will we have to—

There's a whistle like that of a noisy firecracker, then an explosion, far larger than I was expecting, rocks the prison camp, sending flames and shrapnel skyward. The huge lights extinguish without a flicker, and we're plunged into a darkness lit by the dim red-orange glow of Yedys burning. Klaxon sirens blare and we're on the move, jogging a zig-zag path as Manganaro directs us around invisible death. *Serpentine, Sylvy, serpentine.* I stifle an adrenaline chuckle. *Keep it together.*

We reach the wall and almost before I have time to catch my breath, Onai has a secure line and is climbing. Fortunately, I've done some non-mandatory training with the SWAT team, so an ascender would've been familiar to me. Unfortunately, Casilla has already told me ascenders are too slow. The CIA uses a portable electric winch system. Onai has that strapped to his vest and drops its nylon rope shortly after summiting and snipping through the razor wire. I'm third in line, and stare in mute anticipation as Jones and Hardja are zipped up the wall ahead of me.

Then it's my turn and I'm clipping the carabiner to my harness and tugging twice on the rope. I'm launched off the ground and grabbing at the wall as Jones pulls me through the gap in the razor wire. Unclipped, I pull my gun and act as another guard as Casilla, Manganaro, and finally Valcross scale the wall. By the time everyone is up, it's pretty crowded on top of the water tower. As I scan the wall on either side of us, I see the value of the satellite images and Casilla's informants. There's no other structure even close to the wall. We'd have had to scale the wall, and then go over and down again in one go if not for the tower.

The problem now is that the tower itself has nothing else near it and is surrounded by its own fence. Also, the tower is about fifteen feet high with a smooth, rounded top, so I'm wondering how we're going to get down when the thunk of a bolt gun startles me. Onai has a rope secured to a three-fourths-inch-thick bolt now sticking out of the top of the tank and Valcross is sliding down it. We'll go down in reverse order, so I continue to monitor the area while I'm waiting my turn. True to his word, Casilla's distractions are in full force and directed as far from our location as possible. Gunfire echoes inside the walls and I'm temporarily blinded every time a rocket is launched or a grenade goes off.

No guards or other personnel are in sight. The way down

from the tower isn't using the winch, just gravity and a clamp to control the rate of descent...to an extent. When my turn comes, my boots hit the ground hard enough to rattle my teeth. But I've no time to consider the possible crack in my crown as I stumble over to Manganaro, who's making the finishing clips in a hole in the water tower fence. When we're all gathered, guns at the ready, Casilla drops a raised hand and we pour through the hole in the fence. We're a couple hundred feet, at least, from the building with the lab, but we make steady progress dodging between smaller buildings and it only takes us a few minutes to reach it.

The side we're entering from is exposed, so only Valcross rounds the corner. His job is to disable the electronic lock, but I'm in the middle of the pack, so I can't see what's happening. Asking isn't an option; we're on radio silence until we enter the building. But Valcross must not have had any trouble because we're on the move again. I'll be third to last through the door and will lay down cover fire with Onai and Casilla, if needed, for Valcross, Hardja, Jones, and Manganaro. We only pause a few seconds by the door before Valcross throws it open.

Expecting a barrage of gunfire, my breath catches, but all is silent and dark inside. Hardja tosses in a stick which bursts into a brilliant white LED light a moment later. Still nothing happens. Valcross flips up his night-vision goggles, gives the interior a long look, then pitches himself through the door. When nothing happens again, Casilla drops his hand again and Hardja follows suit, then Manganaro.

I'm marveling at our incredible good luck and the smoothness of our entry when a squad of soldiers runs out from between two buildings across from where Casilla, Onai, Jones, and I are still huddled by the open door. At first, I think they're going to pass by without stopping, but then one spots the light coming through the open door and shouts. So much for our luck.

CHAPTER 22

Journal Excerpt Dr. Ahmed Mahadow
Tuesday, January 20th, 2029
RNA Vector Test 47a
Vector 47a shows great promise and WHISP affinity.
Unfortunately, after the death of subjects 477 and 998,
I've recommended that we discontinue testing and focus
on other branches of the project. Dr. Romero and the
rest of the American team disagree and have authorized
duplication of the vector.

I take aim, but Casilla grabs me and pulls me
through the door.

"Incoming!"

Jones lobs a grenade before diving in behind us as Manganaro lays down cover fire. The blast makes me lose my balance,
but I recover and am repositioning to return fire when Casilla
pulls me away from the door and shakes his head.

"Let them take care of that."

In the momentary distraction, someone must have thrown
another grenade, because a second blast sends waves through
my chest and makes my ears ring. Casilla points across the

room, which is a loading area, empty except for a few stray crates. Valcross faces the wall to the right of the door we came in, working at another electronic lock.

"Let's go."

As I follow Casilla, I have time to wonder if the soldiers outside have called for backup and if we'll be exiting through a firing squad. But then we're at the door and I can barely make out Valcross muttering angrily as he untwists and picks at wires. Blowing the door sounded faster and easier when we were planning the assault, but Casilla assured me that most doors had fail-safes that made blowing them a bad idea, and then I'd remembered the wired door at the lab in Upstate New York. Still, time slips away as Valcross fidgets and Manganaro, Hardja, and the others fire out the door.

Finally, Valcross clips a wire and the light on the panel changes from red to green. He punches a fist in the air. "Ha!"

Casilla pats him on the back then turns on his com. "Manganaro! Hardja! Where're we at?"

The reply from Manganaro comes over the com in my ear, "Four or five left. No sign of back-up. Turn and burn?"

"Affirmative, we're in here."

I catch Casilla's eye and raise an eyebrow. "Turn and burn?"

"They're going to lock the door and set explosives for anyone who opens it."

"Ah."

He turns back to Valcross. "You ready?"

Valcross rotates his rifle from his back to his front and steadies it. "Ready."

Casilla speaks into his com again, "Doc, you ready?"

Ben's voice in my ear sends my heart thumping. "Clear visual from all cameras."

Casilla gives a thumb's up to my helmet. "Jones, Hardja, we're headed in. You're our cover."

"Affirmative."

"Got it."

A few moments later, Jones and Hardja join us at the inner door. Images of the aftermath of the raid of the underground lab at the farm invade my brain. Bullet holes, bodies, and blood. A lot of blood.

Casilla holds up three fingers then silently counts them down.

My finger is pressed to the side of my trigger as Valcross flings open the door, but again nothing happens. This time, Casilla tosses in one of the LED sticks. He's crouched, so I peek over his head. Illuminated in the harsh light is a short hallway with a concrete floor and concrete walls leading to a descending staircase. Casilla nods and Valcross is first inside. When he clears the landing, we crowd in and Casilla closes the door behind us. Instantly the cacophony from outside is muffled. Mild claustrophobia takes over as I press against Jones, but Valcross and Hardja are soon moving toward the top of the stairs. All I can think about is the bottleneck of the stairway in front of us and the possible growing platoon of soldiers behind us.

Valcross tosses another light down the stairs. In the muted space of the stairwell, it clatters loudly before rolling to stop at the bottom. I hold my breath. Again, nothing. Valcross peers over the edge.

"Looks like another door with an electronic lock," he says.

Casilla shrugs. "Well?"

Valcross nods and starts down the stairs as Casilla and Jones cover him from the top.

Ben's voice is in my ear again. "There's a small landing down there," he narrates. "Similar lock to the previous. No window in the door. Valcross is working the lock now."

The silence is making me edgy. "Is it possible they don't know about the assault? Could the lab be isolated from the rest of the compound?"

Casilla doesn't look at me. "Not likely. Even if their power doesn't come from the main generators and the bunker is solid enough that nobody felt the explosion, someone would have to be monitoring. Don't be lulled. Get ready for heavy fire."

"Got it," Valcross says over the com.

"Hardja, Harbinger, stay here."

Casilla and Jones follow Valcross down the stairs and all take positions around the door. Casilla counts them down silently on his fingers then Valcross turns the handle but uses his rifle butt to push open the door. Gunfire erupts in earsplitting pops in the sealed stairwell. Casilla and Jones return fire until the door closes again. After a nod from Casilla, Jones drops to the floor and pulls out a small, boxy screen with a length of thick, black cable attached. Jones repositions next to Valcross, Casilla nods again, and Valcross eases the door open the slightest bit. Jones deftly inserts the cable in the gap. Ah, a fiber-optic camera.

Ben's voice is ragged, "At least ten armed guards behind a barricade of crates. Probably more. Visibility's poor."

Casilla breaks in, "Can you see if they're armored or wearing masks?"

"Masks? Um, I don't think so."

Hardja is already handing me a compact gas mask. Casilla and Jones both pull theirs from pockets and are affixing them on their faces as I juggle my gun and the mask, trying to get it on around my goggles and helmet. Hardja snatches it back and presses a catch to show me how to release the strap then hands it back and pulls out his own. With minimum difficulty this time, I get it on and tightened. It has an unpleasant odor and instantly I'm missing the relatively fresh air of the stairwell. Glancing down the stairs, I find the others readying to open the door again. This time, Jones is holding a canister.

Valcross pushes hard on the door. Jones pulls the pin and rolls the canister inside as thick, yellow-tinged smoke pours from the canister as the door swings shut. Maybe thirty seconds go by, then the boom of a detonation echoes on the other side of the door. Immediately, Valcross pushes the door open again as Jones shoves something underneath to keep it open. Casilla lays down cover fire, but I don't think there's any coming from the other side of the open door. What's coming out is the thick, yellow gas, but also regular gray smoke.

Casilla stops shooting. His voice is distorted by his mask. "Doc, report!"

Ben sounds miserable, "Too much smoke. Some of the crates are gone or on fire."

"Any movement?"

"I…I'm sorry, I can't tell."

"Guess there's only one way to find out, then."

Shit. I realize they're going in a moment before Valcross kicks the light forward then crosses the threshold. Gunfire erupts and my heart skips. Jones follows Valcross.

Casilla stays back. "Better?"

Ben comes through again. "Valcross has a good view around the crates now. There are five bodies. I can't see down the hallway. Still too much smoke."

"Jones, check the bodies. Tell me when we're clear." Casilla sounds calm.

A few seconds pass. "Six bodies. Clear."

Casilla motions to Hardja and me. Hardja gestures for me to go first. It seems to me that Onai and Manganaro are taking a long time to join us, but then I remember that Ben can see what they see, so they must be okay. Guess rigging up a bomb properly takes a bit longer than disarming one. I stay to one side of the stairwell as I descend and, at the bottom, crouch on the opposite side of the door from Casilla. When Hardja joins us, Casilla points to him and then me and then to himself. Instead of counting down, he just nods to Hardja, then to me a moment later.

I continue to stick to the right through the door. There's a small room here leading to a large hallway. The makeshift barricade is in shambles and I count the six bodies amidst the wreckage. The gas bomb/grenade was pretty effective; still, now the smoke's made visibility down the hall poor in spite of the fluorescents still functioning. Probably, the surviving guards forced into retreat by the gas are waiting to ambush us around one of the corners. Another bottleneck.

The first door in the hall is about five feet down on the right-hand side. Valcross points at it as the rest of us take up positions at the mouth of the hallway. Casilla glances around then nods to Valcross. Instead of cover fire, Casilla heaves something down the hall and what must be a flash-bang goes off, giving Valcross time to dash to the door. I gather this one has just a normal lock, because he kicks it in then dives for cover as gunfire hits the wall opposite the door.

CHAPTER 23

Recovered File CAW Server
Date: Unknown
WHISP Contagion Test 35
...for over a year with no WHISP formation in any of the
other subjects. This is the longest experiment yet
conducted, and based on the results, the expense and
difficulty of further experiments seems unwarranted.
Exposure to a WHISP alone has not lead to formation of
a WHISP in any known circumstances to date.

I KNOW RIGHT AWAY THAT VALCROSS HAS BEEN HIT.
He rips a packet off his belt, removes a length of cloth, and ties
it around his calf.

"Just a graze," he reports, though his voice is strained.

As Casilla fires high at the open door, Valcross pulls something else from his belt and tosses it into the room. Three,
two... The grenade goes off and debris flies out of the door.
Screaming fills the hall. Valcross is up again, but Casilla shakes
his head.

"Jones. Cover." Casilla darts down the hall to the door,

pauses, pressed against the wall, takes a quick look in, then charges in.

The lack of gunfire does nothing to reassure me. *Come on, Ben, what's happening?* Then a single shot rings out and the screaming ceases.

"Clear," Casilla's tone is neutral.

Bile rises in the back of my throat. Valcross motions us forward and again Hardja signals me to go first. I sprint to the door and find this first room is a surveillance station. Makes sense. Soon Jones and Valcross follow behind me, though Hardja stays at the door. Part of the large bank of screens, and most of the desk, were destroyed by the grenade, but some of the screens still have images. Most are of the surface fighting.

On the floor is the lone guard in a pool of blood. He has a single gunshot to his forehead, but there's also a large chunk of his abdomen missing, intestines spilling through. I'm grateful for the mask.

Though Casilla's last shot was a kindness, there's still a lead weight in my chest. The guard is about Lincoln's age. *Shake is off, Sylvy, you've seen dead kids before.* And I have. Gang recruits mostly, but also a good shake of innocent bystanders. I refocus on the screens, searching for Lincoln, but if there was surveillance inside the lab, it fell victim to the grenade. *Damnit.* A crackle jolts me. The guard's radio. I pick it out of some debris and listen, but there's only static.

Casilla sees me with it and points to it. "Anything?"

"Just static."

He nods. "Good. Coms center's out."

"Might just be damaged."

He turns to the screens, stares at them, and shakes his head. "They'd be coming if they knew we were down here."

Looking at the screens again, he's right. There's no unified force heading toward the building above. Then Casilla ducks under the desk. As I watch, he follows a blue cable to where it enters the wall.

"Valcross!"

Valcross crosses to Casilla and kneels, trying to hide a wince.

Casilla points to the cable. "You stay here and try to get into the feed. Be nice to have more eyes for the Doc to guide us." He stands and activates his com. "Onai, Manganaro, where the fuck are you?"

"Just admiring your work, I think. Some room at the bottom of the stairs?" It's Manganaro.

Hardja waves into the hallway from his post at the door. Onai and Manganaro jog in a little too casually.

Onai takes in the room, then reports, "We left a camera at the inner door. Best to have eyes if someone gets through the burn."

Casilla nods. "Jones. Stay with Valcross until he hacks in or until we get back."

"I heard that." Valcross has a hole cut in the wall now and has pulled out a rat's nest of wires.

Casilla ignores him. "Hardja, Manganaro, Harbinger, Onai, with me. Stay alert. Until Valcross gives us eyes, we're still in the dark."

I nod along with the rest of them. How much time has gone by since we breached the wall? Ten minutes, half an hour? How big can the lab be? How much longer before reinforcements arrive from the nearest city?

"Hey!" Casilla snaps a finger in front of my face. "I *said*, it'd be pretty useful if you could pinpoint where your son is."

I'm about to ask him how he expects me to do that when it's like someone flicks me between my shoulder blades. *Liv. Of course.*

I nod and close my eyes, visualizing Liv floating away from me and down the hall. The now familiar stretching tightness spreads across my back. One door, two doors…. *Lincoln? No, not here.* As I, Liv, reaches the end of the hallway, the pain begins. A sense of something at the brink of tearing. *Just a little farther.* To the right: shapes, people, three of them, huddle, listening, waiting. One is fiddling with a radio, the other two are poised at the ready with machine guns. Behind them, more doors. To the left, two more armed guards. *Which way Liv?* She floats past the guards on the right and someone is peeling the skin from my body. *Am I screaming yet?* A flash, Lincoln's voice. I'm on the floor.

"Sylvy!" Ben's shouting in my ear. "What the hell happened? I thought I saw…. Sylvy, are you okay? Talk to me!"

My mask is off and Manganaro's face is close when I open my eyes.

"She's awake."

"I'm okay, Ben." There's a rasp to my voice. Maybe I did scream. I take a deep breath but regret it. The fetid odor of gore is thick and there's a lingering acidity in the air that burns my lungs.

Manganaro gets an arm under one of mine and Casilla, the other. Together, they haul me to my feet. Jones is still at the door, but Hardja is staring at me, his face a mixture of awe and disgust.

"Well?" Casilla's eyes search my face.

I clear my throat. "End of the hall. Three guards on the right, two on the left. I think we want to go right."

"You think?"

"Sorry, this isn't an exact science."

He huffs. "What about the rest of the rooms in this hall?"

"I didn't feel anyone in them."

"Great." He shakes his head. "Hardja. Clear the rooms when we've dealt with the guards at the end of the hallway, then follow. The Doc will guide you to us."

Hardja stares at me. "We're not just trusting her magic shadow?"

Casilla shoves him hard against the wall. "Hey! We don't have a lot of fucking time here. We're using every available fucking resource! Got it?"

"Yes, Sir."

Casilla lets him go without another word and heads for the door. Manganaro follows him and I follow Manganaro, but Hardja cuts us both off and takes up position just behind Casilla. I don't take it personally. Liv would probably obstruct his view if he were behind me. I fight a sudden urge to check to make sure she's still there, that she didn't get ripped away when she scouted ahead. But I'm okay, so, of course, she's still there.

It's then that my blood runs cold. *If they're researching the WHISP virus here, would they have other anti-WHISP technology here? Shit. Could they catch Liv? Destroy her?*

I don't have time to worry, because Casilla is pulling out another grenade and chucking it down the hall and we're all taking cover on either side of the door frame. Immediately after the blast, Casilla, Hardja, Manganaro, and I rush down the hallway: Casilla and Hardja in front and firing, Manganaro and I covering them from behind. I can't help but peek nervously at each of the two closed doors as we pass. If there is someone hiding in either of them, they could ambush us at any second.

But the doors stay closed and we reach the end of the hallway. Four bodies, one survivor on hands and knees with his gun in front of him. His pleas are in Rubezi, so I don't understand the words, but "Please, I just work here" is written plainly on his face. While Manganaro checks the bodies, Hardja covers Casilla as he speaks to the man. I'm trying to cover both hallways until Manganaro is done with the bodies. The guard stands and removes his shirt and then his pants. Casilla shouts something in Rubezi and the man turns his back to us, gets on the ground, and puts his hands behind his back. Casilla has him hogtied in no time and is shouting into his ear, but the man just keeps repeating the same thing.

Casilla drags him into the hallway we came from. "Hardja, after you clear those rooms, take him to the surveillance room. When Valcross is done hotwiring surveillance, he can continue the interrogation."

Hardja's face contorts with anger, but he only nods. "Yes, sir." Then he heads back down the hall toward the first door past surveillance.

Casilla hits his com. "Doc, we have eyes in the facility yet?"

"Not yet."

"Shit." He turns to me. "You have any better idea than somewhere down this hall?"

"No."

"Wanna do your little trick again?"

No. But I don't have time to answer, because two armed men burst from a door halfway down the right hallway and begin firing.

CHAPTER 24

Encrypted CIA Internal Communication
Re: Rubezikan Situation
Action Assessment: Mandatory
Risk Assessment: Ultra-high
Agent Status: Ghost
Mission Status: Phantom Ops
[Connection terminated]

Casilla and Manganaro are able to duck back down the surveillance room hallway, but I'm not so lucky. These men don't have automatic weapons, so I have a chance to return fire, but I back down the left fork until I find a door that opens. There could be an ambush in this room, too, but I'm a sitting duck in the hallway, so I escape inside. Fumbling for a light switch, the unmistakable sound of a whimper freezes me.

"Sylvy, are you okay? I can't see anything."

Aiming my gun in the direction of the whimper, I slowly slide the fingers of my free hand over the wall until they find the bump of a switch. I breathe in, then flick the light on. I'm in an office lined with books. The whimper came from under the desk. The gunfire in the hallway has ceased. A part of me just wants to pretend I didn't hear anything and leave, but I can't risk getting shot in the back. Keeping my gun pointed at the desk, I step cautiously to the side, one foot crossing behind in a smooth motion until I can see around the desk. The man huddled under it is unarmed. He's around fifty years old, with mousy, graying hair and octagonal-rimmed eyeglasses. In his worn gray suit, he looks like either a head scientist or an administrator.

"Please. Please don't kill me."

English? "Where's my son?"

His brows knit.

"Where's the boy you took from the lab in New York?"

The furrow between his eyes deepens. "He's your son?"

I want to reach under the desk, grab him by the collar, and shake him, but I'm alone in here and bending down would make me vulnerable. I shake my gun at him. "WHERE IS HE!"

The man cowers. "In the lab, I think. He was, earlier. Please! Don't kill me."

"Tell me where the lab is. Down the right hallway? How far?"

"Are you with them?"

Them? "With who?"

He doesn't answer me.

"With who!"

"The CIA."

What? My heart sinks. Crone was right. "I'm here to get my son." I glance at the door and lower my voice. "Were they working with you?"

He nods.

Ben's voice is a whisper in my ear, "Sylvy, what's he talking about?"

I press the button on the com to only talk to Ben. "Where are Manganaro and Casilla?"

"Um, they were chasing the shooters, but they went into a room with an electronic lock. It might be a lab, they're working the lock."

It might be a lab. Lincoln. I don't know what's going on, but I have to get to Lincoln. The man under the desk is shaking, but I don't have time for him. This could be a terrible mistake, but I don't have a choice. "Stay here. Stay quiet."

He nods. "Thank you."

I think about the talk of us blowing the lab on our way out and I shake my head. "Don't." I go back to the door and peer out. The hallway's quiet. "Where are they, Ben?"

"Down the right hallway and around the corner. But, Sylvy, why did he say he was working with the CIA? What's going—" He cuts off.

"Ben?"

"Sylvy, you have to get there right now. Now! It's Lincoln! But shit!"

"Ben? Ben!"

No reply.

I leave the office at a sprint, not bothering to check down the surveillance hall when I pass it. Farther down the right hallway, the echo of raised voices reaches me. *Is that Lincoln? I'm coming!* My chest burns from remnant gas bomb fumes, but I'm almost to the corner. I catch myself at the last possible moment before rounding it and flick on the general com.

"Manganaro, Casilla? I'm coming around the corner to you. Don't shoot me."

I round the corner low, just in case. Manganaro is guarding a door a few feet down the hall. He points his gun at me. "Stay there."

The shouting is easier to make out here. One of the voices is definitely Lincoln. I advance on Manganaro. "Or what?"

For a brief moment, I think I've made a terrible mistake. Something subtle about his eyes tells me that he would shoot me if he thought it was necessary. Fortunately, he doesn't because he lets me brush past him into the room. *What the hell?* Casilla is pointing his gun at Lincoln, but Lincoln has a gun of his own aimed at Casilla. Behind Lincoln, five men in white coats are huddled in a sealed glass laboratory area. I pull out my gun and aim it at Casilla.

"I won't let you— Mom?" Lincoln's grip on the pistol wavers as he sees me, but then he refocuses on Casilla and it steadies again. "What are you doing here?"

Casilla spots me out of the corner of his eye. "Harbinger, put the gun down."

"You first."

Lincoln swallows hard. "Are you with them?"

"I'm here with the CIA to rescue you, so I'm wondering why you and Casilla are aiming guns at each other."

"The CIA made the virus. They didn't come to rescue me, they came to get it back."

Casilla shakes his head a fraction. "Kid, you've got your wires crossed. I don't know who told you what, but those men behind you are terrorists working with ex-CIA operatives to murder a lot of innocent people. Just tell me where to find them."

Lincoln ignores Casilla. "The CIA came to the Rubezi after so many of their people got WHISPs all at once. They offered to work with them to find a cure. But they weren't looking for a cure, not really. After they took them to the laboratory in New York, the Rubezi scientists accidentally created a WHISP virus. They knew it was dangerous, but they thought it could hold the key to a cure, so they were trying to study it. Then the CIA released it and forced them to work on making it better, more virulent. When the task force raided the lab, the Rubezi were able to escape from the CIA and fly home."

My brain is whirling. "Why did they kidnap you? Why did they kill the chief?"

Lincoln's face falls. "That was an accident. They didn't know who to trust, but they thought that since I had a WHISP, I couldn't be with the CIA. They told me they were trying to find a cure and hide the virus from the CIA. Some of the reports I'd been going over supported what they said, so I went with them."

"You went with them?"

Casilla flinches.

"Don't move!" Lincoln's arms are trembling.

"Kid, we don't have time for this. Put the gun down."

My mind is reeling. My cop sense tells me Casilla's a good guy, but that doesn't mean he's doing the right thing for the right reasons. I take a step toward him. "Why are you really here, Casilla? What's the primary mission goal here? Find the virus, kill all the witnesses?"

"No. It's to find the virus and—"

"Sylvy, look out!" Ben's voice shouts in my earpiece.

Gunfire erupts and my heart stops, but it's not Lincoln and Casilla firing at each other. I turn and Manganaro falls into the room, his face covered with blood.

"Get back!" Casilla spins away from Lincoln to face the door.

I don't know what's happening, but since he's no longer aiming his pistol at my son, I spin toward the door and leap in front of Lincoln. The only cover not inside the glass-encased laboratory is a single lab bench in front of it. I point to it.

"Get behind there!"

Lincoln grabs my shoulder. "Not without you."

I dive with him as gunfire erupts through the door. As I'm falling, I spot Casilla returning fire, but one arm hangs limply at his side. He makes his way to us, firing as he walks, but he's hit again in the leg and once more in the abdomen before he makes it to cover. He falls more than sits next to me and presses his back against the cabinets.

"Shit." For once, all of his confidence has drained from his face.

I flick on my com. "Ben, what's going on?"

"Something's wrong, Sylvy, someone's coming."

"Ben, get out of there! Do you hear me? Get out!"

Lincoln grabs my hand. "Is that Dad?"

CHAPTER 25

Excerpt Personal Diary: Dr. Ahmed Mahadow
Saturday, February 2nd, 2030
"O Allah forgive us, what have we done?"

My mouth is too dry to reply. Swallowing hard,
I nod once.

"Come out, come out, wherever you are!" The taunt comes
from the hallway. "Oh, Agent Casilla, is it? Never had the pleasure, sadly. I'd just toss in a bunch of grenades and kill you all,
but we're on a bit of a tight schedule, as you well know, so...."

The door slams shut.

I look at Casilla. "Turn and burn?"

He nods. "Probably."

Cautiously, I cross to where Manganaro is sprawled and
check for a pulse. It's there, but weak. I drag him back to the
cover of the bench. About halfway back, Lincoln is there helping. My head is spinning and I can't catch my breath. We're
trapped in this lab, Casilla and Manganaro are down, Ben is...
hopefully, gone. I flick on the open channel.

"Hardja, Valcross? Does anyone read me?"

Silence.

Okay. No help is coming. We have to figure this out on our own. I glance at the glass surrounding the inner lab and spot fine wires running through it. Safety glass, good. First things first. "Lincoln, can you get those scientists to let us into the lab? The glass might protect us from the blast from the door."

To his credit, he doesn't ask "what blast," just nods, runs to the glass door, and gestures while talking through it to the men on the other side.

"Do you believe I'm not involved now?" Casilla wheezes.

"So, rogue CIA agents are responsible for the virus?"

He coughs. "Yes."

"You were sent to neutralize them."

"And the terrorists, and the lab, and recover the virus, and your son."

Just one problem. "But they weren't here."

"Guess not."

It's coming together now. "The Rubezi broke away from them in New York when they tried to force them to work on the virus. Probably thought they'd be safe back here in their own country, only we chased them, and the rogue CIA agents followed us."

"Looks like." He coughs again, but I've little sympathy at the moment.

"You knew we'd be up against ex-CIA agents and you didn't tell me?"

"Was classified."

Lincoln's convinced the scientists to open the inner lab door. I reach down to help Casilla up. "Was a dick move."

Casilla's able to stand, so we make our way over to the protection of the glass enclosure. He winces and grunts, but otherwise doesn't express his pain. Once Lincoln helps me get him down near the back of the lab, I try to get a better look at his wounds, but he shakes his head.

"I'll live...if we get out of here."

I nod. "Let the scientists help you if they can. I know they're not those kind of doctors, but there must be, at least, a first aid kit around here."

There's a hand on my shoulder and I reach for my gun. One of the scientists backs up rapidly, trips over his own feet, and bangs against a piece of equipment on a stand.

Easy Harbinger. "Sorry. You startled me."

The man nods shakily then speaks in broken English. "I want to tell you we are sorry. Sorry for the virus. We did not mean to make it. Did not mean to give it to them. Did not know they would use it. We thought they were, um, good guys."

"I get that." I stand.

I'm not sure how to accept his apology. We're still in an underground lab at a prison camp where they're experimenting on people and we really don't have time to "hug it out." Lincoln and some of the other scientists have gone back for Manganaro and are now hoisting him onto a counter. I move to Lincoln's side.

"How is he?"

"Not good."

One of the scientists is placing a rolled up lab coat under his head while another cuts away fabric from Manganaro's shirt. He was wearing body armor, but the bullet penetrated his abdomen just under it. A third scientist brings over a med kit and places a wad of gauze over the wound. Casilla waddles over to stand next to the scientist applying the gauze.

"Here, let me do it." Casilla reaches over and presses his hands against the gauze as a red stain blossoms through.

Manganaro's skin is chalky. I swallow hard. "Is he going to make it?"

Casilla tapes the gauze in place. "If we can make it to a medical facility in thirty minutes or less." He coughs into his hand and it comes away bloody.

I put a hand on his arm. "Shouldn't you sit down, at least?"

"Shouldn't you be working to get us out of here?" he snaps.

Step one of my plan was to get everyone into the shelter of the tempered glass area of the lab. Check. Step two. I turn to Lincoln.

"What's the code for the outer door?"

Lincoln opens his mouth, but Casilla butts in, "Are you crazy? You'll blow yourself up!"

Casilla's lack of confidence is a little insulting.

"Not me." I hitch my thumb over my shoulder. "Her. Hopefully."

His face turning into a mask, Casilla glances at Liv then busies himself with Managanro's wound again. "How does that work?"

"Well, the keypad will be giving off some electromagnetic radiation and I've seen WHISPs manipulate electronic things before."

"Manipulate?"

I clear my throat. "Throw, but same principle." *I hope.* I look back at Lincoln.

He rattles off, "Three, three, nine, two, nine, three."

"Three, three, nine, two, nine, three," I repeat.

He nods.

I cross to the inner door and close it. "Everybody take cover."

One or two of the scientists look to Lincoln, clearly confused, but they don't move. Then Casilla barks at them in Rubezi and they all rush to the back of the lab and get behind a counter. Casilla scoops up Manganaro and shelters behind the closer counter. I join him there and Lincoln stays with us. I want to tell him to get farther back, but he won't listen, so I don't bother. I close my eyes. *Okay, Liv. Time to bust us out of here.* I "aim" her at the outer door and try to picture the keypad on the other side. *Three, three, nine, two, nine, three. Three, three, nine, two, nine, three.* After the familiar tug at my back, she drifts to the glass and I feel a jolt akin to a kiss from an electric fence.

"Ow! Shit!"

Lincoln's hand is on my arm. "What's wrong, Mom?"

"Is this glass shielded from WHISPs somehow?"

He face crumples. "Yeah. It is."

"Dammit." Nothing for it then. I rise and walk to the door. I don't ask for the code, because I don't want to confuse the two. "Lincoln, open this door and close it behind me and get back to cover."

He comes to me but doesn't punch in the code. "If I close the door, you won't be able to get back inside before—"

"I wouldn't have time even if I leapt inside as she pressed the last button. I'll shelter behind the bench out there. I'll be fine."

He sets his jaw. "Do it from the open door."

"Lincoln, please. We don't have time for this. I don't even know if this will work in the first place. I don't want to make it harder with any interference."

He hesitates.

"They're getting the virus right now. They'll blow the building when they leave."

He takes in a sharp breath then nods. One hand reaches for the keypad, but with his other arm, he hugs me. "Be careful."

I hug him back. "Always am."

The door opens and I push through it, then shut it behind me. Taking cover behind the outer lab bench, I quickly send Liv out again. This time she floats right over to the door. Her ghostly gray fingers skim over the buttons of the keypad, once, twice...*Three, three, nine, two, nine, three. Come on, Liv. You can do it.*

CHAPTER 26

Excerpt Letter from Dr. Hu Litz to Gretchen Litz (Translated)

I think I've created something horrible. I didn't know what was happening until after the Department of Defense confiscated my research, but by then it was too late. We'd already sold the technology. I shouldn't be telling you any of this and I'm not sure if this letter will even reach you, but if it does, I want you to know that I'm sorry. I never meant for any of this to happen.

KABOOM ISN'T AT ALL WHAT A BOMB SOUNDS LIKE, and it doesn't adequately describe the sensory overload nor the sensation of the bomb's blast wave ripping through you. Nevertheless, that's the word that popped in my head when the door exploded in a bright, hot flash that propelled a large chunk of the metal door over me and into the wall of the enclosed lab behind me. Glass broke but didn't shatter, and I let out the breath I'd been holding. I'm alive. I'm okay, I think. Examining the cabinets in front of me for penetrating shrapnel, I then examine myself. I'm covered with dust, but no blood. Lucky.

Before standing up, I peer around the corner to check if

anyone has come running, but there's just a nice-sized hole in the wall where the door used to be. Still, I train my gun on the hole as I back to the inner lab door, stepping over the charred remains of the outer lab door. Lincoln's there and opens it for me. I step inside, and mostly close the door, but don't take my eyes off the hole. Someone had to have heard that.

"Is everyone okay in here?" I spare a glance at the door and the surrounding glass walls. They're opaque with rectangular cracks, but it doesn't look like any of the shrapnel got through.

"Yeah. You did it."

Do I detect a hint of awe in my son's voice? "Okay. You stay here, coms are down, but I'm hoping one of the good guys heard that blast and is on the way."

"Where're you going?"

"I'm thinking if the"—*rogue CIA agents* is just too much to say—"bad guys had the virus already they wouldn't have bothered to lock us in. They would've just quietly left and blown us up on the way out. If it's not in here, where is the virus?" I glance at Lincoln. "And why didn't you destroy it?"

"It's not that easy. It's like a prion, and besides, it may still hold some clues about a cure."

Ben was right. "Okay, okay. Where is it?"

"I don't know. Rahim, where is the virus right now?"

One of the scientists approaches. "It is in the other lab. The biosecurity lab."

"That's where they're headed, then. Does it have a similar lock to this one?" Oh, please let it have a retinal scanner or something.

"Yes."

Shit.

"But also a handprint scanner."

"Casilla, can they get around that or do they need a hand?"

He's positioning Manganaro on a makeshift gurney with the help of another scientist. His voice is weaker than it was before the bomb went off. "It takes a long time to get around. Much easier to use a hand."

Then why haven't they come back for one? Did they find the scientist I left cowering under his desk? "How many people not in this room would have access?"

Rahim scans the room. "Two."

Another scientist joins the conversation. "Where is Ali? He was supposed to be here."

My eyes find Casilla's and I know he's thinking the same thing. Maybe the split between the Rubezi and the ex-CIA wasn't as clear cut as it seemed, and if they have easy access to the lab with the virus, there's no time to waste.

Casilla nods at me. "These guys are highly trained and hate WHISPs. Be careful."

I load a fresh magazine in my gun. "I will." I turn to Lincoln. "Follow Casilla's lead. He'll get you out of here." I give him a fierce but brief hug. "I love you." As I'm heading back out the lab door, Lincoln is on my heels. My heart cringes to have him out in the open. "What are you doing?"

He lifts his gun. "I can't let you go alone."

This is a terrible idea. If we had more time, I might be able to convince him not to come with me. He has no training and I don't even know if he's ever shot a gun. He'll be a distraction... but he'll also be someone to cover my back. *Oh Liv, what if I can't protect him?* I move to the edge of the hole and motion for him to flank the other side of it.

"Have you ever shot a gun before?" The hallway is clear.

"Once. Do you remember my friend Sven? His family took me hunting upstate."

Hunting? You told me you went camping. Not the time. "Which way is the other lab?"

"Right, then left, then right again, about halfway down the hall."

"Okay. Stay close behind me. Watch our backs, but if you

see someone, just grab me and get down. It might be one of the good guys."

"Okay." His voice wavers just a little.

As we slide along the wall toward the first junction, I send Liv out ahead. This time, the pull is painful from the very beginning. *Are we getting tired?* Around the corner, the hallway is deserted. Good enough for now. She snaps back and the pain evaporates. Maybe it's time to give her a break and do things the old-fashioned way. We round the first corner and I switch to the other wall and slide along that until we reach the next bend. Crouching, I lean forward and peer out. There's two men with machine guns at the far corner I don't recognize, one on each side. They aren't dressed like guards. I pull my head back and put my finger to my lips. Then I hold up two fingers then point to my gun. Lincoln nods like he understands. But I need to know how many more of them are around the corner. Taking out two offenders is a lot different than taking out six. Or twelve. But really, if they had that many, we'd all be dead by now.

I send Liv out again, but there's definitely something wrong. I don't know if it's the deeper lab's WHISP protection or if I'm just not used to using her like this, but my back and my head immediately erupt with pain. She recoils and sweat trickles down my forehead. Lincoln glances at me, concern in his eyes. Okay, options: one, shoot first and count later, or two....

One it is. I hold up three fingers to Lincoln and count them down, an empty feeling growing in my stomach. Keeping low to stay out of their line of sight, I drop my last finger, lean out again, and aim for knees, two shots to the left then two shots to the right. Ducking back into cover, a strangled cry lets me know at least one bullet hit home. Return fire lets me know I didn't cause enough injury to either man, and now that they know someone's here...fuck. I'm not used to perps returning fire with grenades, but if Casilla's team is any indication..., I grab Lincoln and sprint for the opposite corner, hoping the bad guys aren't boxing us in. We make it round the other corner just as the grenade goes off in the hallway behind us.

I can't even look at Lincoln right now, so I check our surroundings instead. No one behind us. Small favors. I lean forward just enough to spy around the corner. They'll have to come check to see—another grenade bounces into view—or not. I pin Lincoln against the wall with my free hand and duck back. The second grenade going off jars my teeth. Dumb, Harbinger, dumb. They can just keep advancing, tossing grenades as they go. Fuck. There's a tug on my sleeve. I turn my head and Lincoln is pointing to my belt where six grenades are strapped. I'd forgotten about them.

Nodding, I pull one off and give it a quick once over. My heart is pounding in my ringing ears. I've never thrown one before, but how hard can it be? Pin, release, it looks just like the ones on TV. I pull the pin and heave it down the twice exploded hallway; hopefully, all the way to the end. *Three*— Lincoln covers his ears and I shield my face—*two, one*. My grenade goes off and produces a scream. Good, but we could be lobbing grenades back and forth while the bad guys are taking the back way out of here. I cup Lincoln's ear with my hands to talk to him.

"Is there another way out that way?" Hopefully, he under- stands me.

He nods.

Of course, there is.

The screaming has stopped. We're out of time, we have to move forward. But it's suicide. It's also millions of lives at stake. "Okay. We're gonna have to go fast. Stay behind me."

Lincoln's eyes are wide, but he nods.

I peer around the corner one last time and get ready to run. If I can just get close enough, they won't be able to lob grenades. The hallway is clear save for smoke from smoldering chunks of wall and ceiling. I hold up three fingers again and then two and then one and then—someone grabs me from behind and pulls me back. I've got my gun under his chin before I recognize Hardja. Lincoln's face is pasty, but he moves to point his gun at Hardja. I shake my head and pull my gun out from under his chin.

"Where have you been?"

He grits his teeth. "Busy." He pushes me back to get a look around the corner, then leans back. "So have you."

"One down, but they may be on the move. There's another exit."

He nods. Looks at me, then more doubtfully at Lincoln. "You stay here. We'll take it from here, kid."

"I'm not leaving her," Lincoln hisses.

Hardja shrugs. "More likely, you'll get us all killed than be helpful, but your choice." He turns back to me. "Ready?"

I give Lincoln one pleading look. *He's right. Stay here.* Then I nod. Hardja doesn't count us down. He just moves.

CHAPTER 27

Encrypted CIA Internal Communication (partial)
...at least three security breaches at the highest levels.
These breaches coincide with global WHISP activity and
with seven agents going off grid. Protocol Asunder has
been initiated....

I'M RIGHT BEHIND HIM, EXPECTING ANOTHER
grenade blast, but it doesn't come. In my peripheral vision,
Lincoln follows us out and past the ragged hole that used to be
the corner of the hallways. Hardja fires his machine gun as he
goes, but the hallway with the sentry is now empty except for
two bloody pools and a blood trail. Hardja doesn't even pause
until he reaches the corner where the sentry was, and then fires
down the hallway without looking. Then he pauses, but
nothing happens. He pulls out a mirror on a short stick and
uses it to see around the corner.

"Shit." He pockets the mirror and picks up the gun again.
"No one."

We're too late.

He takes off again. As we run past the open lab door, we
have to leap over a man in a lab coat with a bullet hole in his

head. It's not the man from under the desk, but whether a traitor or a victim, we'll probably never know. As we near the end of the hallway, Hardja slows. I'm not sure why until voices penetrate the hammering of blood in my ears.

"Hurry up!"

"Shut up! I thought I heard something."

A head pokes out from the end of the hall, and Hardja fires. I do the first thing that comes to mind and reach for a grenade, but then realize we'd have no cover from the explosion. I grab Hardja's waist and pull him back with me to the open lab door, thankful that the dead scientist's foot prevented it from closing. Lincoln ducks inside then me, and then Hardja gets the idea and lobs his own grenade down the hall before diving back inside the lab for cover. I never thought I'd get used to the sound of grenades going off, but this one seems a little routine. Hardja is out the door and running again almost before the shrapnel hits the floor. I look back once to make sure Lincoln's okay, then follow him out—and get blasted back as a retaliation grenade goes off almost in front of us.

Even as I'm falling backwards into Lincoln, I know Hardja's dead. There's just something cut-string in the way he falls. A second later, shrapnel pierces my right thigh and my right arm. White hot pain explodes through the right side of my body. But it could be much worse. Hardja took the brunt of the grenade and, in effect, shielded me. I only hope I shielded Lincoln even better from the blast. He's at my side now.

"Mom!"

"I'm okay." Leaning to my left, I sit up and whip my head toward the door. "Shut that."

He leaps up to comply but looks out at Hardja's body. "What about—"

"He's dead."

Lincoln squats to push the dead scientist's foot out of the

way, but then stands and takes cover to the side. "We can't close it. I don't know the code. We'll be locked inside."

"Shit. Okay. Keep lookout." I examine my arm first. My hand is numb and my gun is nowhere close. It must've been knocked from my hand when I hit the floor. A piece of metal is protruding from a weeping wound close to my elbow. Hopefully, the numbness in my hand is just due to a tweaked nerve and not a severed one. It's dangerous to remove the shrapnel as I could nick nerves and blood vessels in the process, but leaving it in isn't an option, so I bite down on my collar, grab the sharp metal with the cuff of my left sleeve, and yank.

"Mom! Mom!"

I'm lying down again. Must've blacked out for a second, but the shrapnel shard is out and digging into my left hand. I sit up again and examine the wound. It's oozing, but not spurting blood. Good sign. I really should wrap it, but there isn't time for such life-saving frivolity. I can move my arm, if not my hand, that'll have to be enough right now. My leg is bleeding a little more freely and has a nice puddle of red underneath it, but there's nothing sticking out of it, so I attempt standing. Pain floods up from screaming muscles and I have to bite my tongue to keep from voicing those screams, but the leg holds my weight. Good enough. Considering my options, I hobble over to Lincoln. I can hold and fire a weapon from my left hand. I know this from a dare during my days as a stupid cadet with something to prove. But I'm not willing to stake both Lincoln's and my life on that ability.

Holding up a hand, I lean out and scan the hallway, then pull back and listen. It's eerily quiet. We could always just head back the way we came in. Hardja came from that direction, so it must be secure. Gazing into my son's eyes, I know I've got what I came for, and probably the bad guys got away. Probably they're out the back door and disappearing into the night...

with the virus. There's also the possibility that they murdered Ben.

"Lincoln, give me your gun. I need you to get Hardja's machine gun. I'll show you how it works."

He hands me his pistol and I take it awkwardly with my left hand and reposition it using my right wrist.

"What's wrong with your hand?"

"Don't worry about that. It'll be fine. Focus. I'll cover you. You'll have to cut the strap. There's a knife in my right pocket."

He reaches in and fishes out the pocketknife but hesitates. My heart is screaming in my head. *What if they lob another grenade?* They could. I could be forced to watch Lincoln, like Hardja, crumple like a ragdoll to the floor.

"Wait."

Come on, Liv. One more time. I try to push her out, but there's a similar zap as in the other lab. "Ah!"

"What is it?"

I shake my head. "I'm trying to get Liv to check around the corner, but the lab must be shielded." *Get ready, Liv.* Taking in a deep breath, I step out into the hallway and send her down to the corner. The pain drops me to my knees, and my right leg gives out. I land on my right arm and my vision goes white, but just before it does, Liv shows me four bodies, no one standing. Four bodies and a door with blood on the handle.

"Mom!" Lincoln's lifting me off the concrete and trying to drag me back into the lab.

"No. I'm..." *Am I?* Everything hurts and a migraine is making my eyes water and my stomach twist. "I'm okay." I push him toward Hardja. "It's clear, get the gun."

While Lincoln wrestles with Hardja's corpse, I use the wall to get to my feet. This time, I didn't lose my gun, so I adjust it again in my left hand. It's all wrong there. Lincoln hoists the automatic up and I point at it with my limp right hand. "That's the safety. Be careful, it's off right now. That's the trigger. Keep your finger off of it until I tell you. Put your hands there and there. Yes. Good. Okay, let's go."

Jogging isn't an option with my leg, so we settle on a fast walk. When we reach the corner, I don't hesitate. I know the men are dead. I trust Liv. We step over bodies until we're at the door.

"Please tell me you know this code."

Lincoln nods and my shoulders sag with relief as he types it in and the light turns green. As I turn the handle, I pray they didn't have time for another turn and burn here. The door opens and nothing explodes. I let out a breath, and Lincoln makes a small animal squeak beside me. Ever so slowly, I crack the door and peek through. The stairwell is empty and quiet, but I'm not taking any more chances. I ease Lincoln's pistol through the crack, shoot up the stairs, pull the gun back, and shut the door.

"What're you doing?"

In retrospect, they probably wouldn't drop grenades down a stairwell they were still in, but I need to be sure. When nothing happens for ten seconds, I have Lincoln reenter the code. This time, I open the door a crack and shout.

"Hey! NYPD! Put your weapons on the ground!" It's reflex. My voice echoes against the concrete, but there's no response, neither verbal nor gunfire. "Okay, let's go."

Leading with Lincoln's pistol, I enter the stairwell and hobble as fast as I can up the steps. The railing sports several bloody handprints. By the time we're at the top, my leg is screaming in protest and the narrow space is spinning around me. I close my eyes and lean against the door. "Where does this lead?"

"The WHISP cells."

My eyes fly open. "What?"

"This is the part of the prison where they keep research volunteers. Easy to get them in and out."

And they just went in there with the WHISP virus. *Shit.* No time to rest. "Open it."

Lincoln keys in the code and I have him stand behind the door while I flank the other side. He opens it wide. Nothing happens, and there's no sound save muffled sirens. I peer into the room. It's an antechamber with biohazard suits hanging along one wall.

"Clear." I cross to the other side. The door here has a small window. I peek through it. The other side could be a hallway in Rikers, one of the security checkpoints before a cellblock. At the end of it are two men, one aiming an automatic in our direction and the other typing in the access code. "Fuck." I duck down and motion Lincoln to the other side of the door.

"What?"

"They're out there. I don't know if they saw me." I risk another quick glance through the window. The men are gone.

CHAPTER 28

Excerpt FBI Sealed Criminal File: Rachel Chester
The question still remains: what made her WHISP different? Was it her underlying psychosis that somehow fueled her WHISP? Or was it some environmental factor such as her work in a facility with a particle accelerator? Or did she somehow exercise her WHISP to strengthen it?

"THEY'RE GONE. OPEN IT."

Lincoln punches in the numbers and the access light turns green. When I open this door, the sirens are now wailing above a cacophony of screams and shouts, the sounds of a prison riot. I sort of gallop-skip down the hallway, but slow near the door. This one has a window in it, too. On the other side is a cellblock, but I can't see far enough down either side to see where the men went.

"I can't see them. Open it." Thank goodness, Lincoln has a head for numbers. I've lost count of how many doors we've been through, at this point.

When the door clicks open, I ease it wider to see down the

hall to the left and gunfire erupts from the right. *Shit!* I jerk my head back before I get a hole in my skull. *Would they throw another grenade in here?* Maybe not. It could blast open cell doors, trigger a lock down. I kneel on my good knee and position myself to shoot down the hall, then nod to Lincoln to open the door. When he does, I lean forward just enough to sight down the hall, but I don't see anyone.

"Shit."

Getting up, I check both sides of the hallway again before limping out into the cellblock. Bodies are in most of the nearby cells, but not from the virus. Blood and bullet holes cover the victims. *Dammit.* Body after body as we pass each cell. Lincoln stops in front of one.

"She was nice. Spoke some English."

I nod and gently nudge him on. When we reach the end of the block, I'm expecting more carnage, but they must not have had as much time here, because there are live WHISPers in the cells all pointing in one direction. I incline my head in thanks to them, get down on my good knee again, and peer around the corner, but this one is a short hallway and they've already passed through it.

"Shit."

Rising, I try to hobble faster.

"Look out!" One of the prisoners shouts, but it's too late.

The men ambush us from a side passage. One knocks me to the ground and stomps on my gun hand with steel-toed boots. My middle finger snaps and I drop Lincoln's gun as pain slices up my arm. Behind me, the automatic clatters from Lincoln's hands to the floor. My assailant kicks me hard in the ribs for good measure. Another explosion of pain indicates one of my ribs is now bruised, maybe even cracked with a hairline fracture.

"Get up."

I can't figure out why they're not shooting us, so I comply as best I can. Pain making my movements too slow for him, he grabs my bad arm and hauls me up, pinning it behind me then placing the muzzle of his pistol under my chin.

"Try anything and I'll kill your son."

Lincoln's assailant has him by the throat and has a pistol resting against his temple.

I must register at least a hint of surprise on my face, because the man continues, "Oh, yeah. I know who you are, Detective. You and your whole family. Didn't think we'd be able to take you alive, but lucky us. Now we get to figure out why the fuck you didn't die before." He waves his gun at Lincoln. "And wonderboy here is gonna help us." He sticks the gun back under my chin. "But first things first."

He kicks my bad leg out from under me and I hit the concrete in a bone-jarring heap, too many agonies vying for my attention to focus on any one. I blink tears out of my eyes and watch him pull a vial from a pouch. The tink of glass on glass tells me it's one of several. Staring down at me, he smiles, opens the vial, and splashes some into my face. My eyes find Lincoln's. His are wide with terror. The man then flings some at the nearest WHISPer prisoners. He drops the vial and crushes it under his boot. These are close quarters. *How long will it take the virus to spread? Can they quarantine those prisoners in time?*

"Right, now, where were we?"

In a movie, this would be the time that the cavalry would show up—Casilla and Valcross, and, while we're at it, heck, Ben, too. Rescuing the damsel. The man kicks me again, knocking off my helmet and sending white hot pain into my brain, and still no cavalry. The man hauls me to my feet again by my hair. *Liv, a little help here?* Nothing. She must be tapped out. I look at Lincoln, and his expression has changed subtly.

He's got the same look Ben gets when he's deep in the throes of figuring out something complex. Oh, no, Lincoln. Don't do anything—

The sprinklers go off drenching us instantly in cold water. It's just enough distraction, and my captor is still sputtering when I send my left elbow into his throat. As I spin, I bring up my right arm and use it as a baton to knock the gun out of his hand. The injury doesn't leave me with enough strength to manage it, so I wrap his arm with both of mine and drop to the ground, letting gravity and my dead weight pull him off balance. He wobbles but recovers quickly and throws me off without dropping the gun.

Bang!

"Lincoln!"

In slow motion, I turn my head. My heart, my lungs, my soul, everything is collapsing in on me. But Lincoln is up and holding a gun in his hands. He shoots again. Then again. Then again. The man I was fighting drops to his knees, then falls face down on the concrete floor. My gaze returns to Lincoln, and then behind him. My knife, the one Lincoln used to cut Hard-ja's gun strap, is protruding from the other man's throat. *Good boy.* Lincoln rushes toward me.

I raise my hands. "No! Don't touch me! Don't get too close. The virus!"

Lincoln waves his hand around. "Is probably splashing all over me right now."

Fuck. I let him help me to my feet. *We can cure him later, right Liv?* Maybe I get a small positive sensation, but it's hard to tell with all the blinding pain. I lean against the bars of a cell and point to the dead man.

"Get the virus."

Lincoln retrieves the pouch. I take it from him with my semi-functional left hand and stow it in the med kit on my belt.

"Get us out of here."

Leaning heavily on Lincoln, we make our way out of the cell block. I try not to make eye contact with the WHISPers we pass, but none are at their cell doors begging to be let out. That and the lack of guards here bother me, but we have to get out and find Casilla. If the Rubezi soldiers of Yedys find us, I doubt they'll listen to a very complicated story about us attacking and breaking into their prison camp, which was mostly a misunderstanding. *Still.*

"Do you know how to open the cells?"

"Only the ones in this block. Why?"

I gesture around. "We should let them out."

Lincoln shakes his head. "They don't want to get out."

"Lincoln, they're being experimented on in a prison camp."

"Mom, I told you, they're volunteers. Many of them came here for protection. They were hunted outside. Sometimes by their own families."

"Oh." My head is spinning again. The WHISPer prisoners could all be infected with the WHISP virus now, and with so many WHISPers in Rubezikan, this could start the epidemic we so narrowly avoided in New York. Still, it feels wrong just to leave. "Shouldn't we, at least, still give them the option?"

Lincoln holds my gaze, then nods. "Okay."

Another few turns and we reach a security door. Lincoln pulls out a card and swipes it across the pad then turns a crank to open the cell block doors while I wedge the door open with a rag torn from my ragged shirt. We don't have time to look back down the cell block and see what choice the prisoners are making, but at least they have one. Two more corners and we reach an outer door. Looking through the little window in the door, I try to get my bearings, but it's dark outside.

"Where's the water tower from here?"

Lincoln thinks for a moment. "Left. To our left."

"How far?"

"Maybe a block?"

A block. Okay, not too far. We can do this. I crack the door and listen, but all the shouting and explosions are far off and farther between then they were. *Good.* As we exit and stumble over to the next building, I just hope Lincoln doesn't buckle under my weight. The pain has levelled off to a manageable agony, but it's getting more difficult to focus. Definitely blood loss and maybe the first signs of shock. *Almost there, Sylvy.* Maybe Casilla will be waiting for us at the water tower.

———

I'M NOT SURE HOW MUCH TIME HAS PASSED WHEN WE finally crawl through the hole in the fence around the tower. Five minutes, ten? The sky is dark again, no explosions painting it red, yet there's soft light around us. Awareness comes like a smack to the face. There are lights. They've gotten the generators working again, or at least some of them. *Shit. Shit. Shit.* And, of course, no one is waiting for us. The only saving grace is that the rope is still there to climb up. Climb. Up. I try to close my right hand and watch my fingers wiggle, despair growing like an alien in my chest. I reach for the rope with my left hand and try to get a grip without being able to bend my broken middle finger, but there is no way the flimsy grip can hold my weight.

Now, my eyes prickle. Turning to Lincoln, I dig the pouch with the virus vials out of my med kit and press it into his hand. "Take this. Climb the tower, then use the rope to get down the other side. Go straight away from the wall for about a half mile, then turn left and go about three miles." I pull the GPS unit from around my neck and try to put it around his, but he stops me.

"What are you talking about? You're coming with me."

"Lincoln, I can't climb." I hold up my hands, the right flops on my wrist, the left's middle finger juts at an obscene angle. "There's no time, you have to go without me."

"No!"

"They'll come back for me." I know that's not true, but Lincoln never heard the talk about there not being a failure protocol.

"No. There must be another way."

The silence around us is suddenly deafening. I lower my voice to a whisper, "Sweetie, you have to do this for me. Please. I'll be fine. I'll hide until you come back."

He shakes his head. "I'm not leaving you, Mom. I'll climb up and then pull you up."

I take his head in my hands as best I can. "There isn't time. You—" A sharp tap on my shoulder makes me jump nearly out of my skin. Reaching for my gun with my left hand, I spin and put my body in front of Lincoln. But there's nobody there. My heart still racing, I scan left and right. *What the Hell?* And that's when I see it. There's a hole blown in the wall behind the water tower. It's not big, but certainly big enough for a person to squeeze through. *Thank you, Liv.*

"What is it?"

Turning to face Lincoln, I allow myself a smile. "Our ticket. Come on."

As I'm pushing him back through the hole in the water tower fence, shouts echo through a gap in the buildings to our right. *Mother of shit. Not now. We're so close.* We could hide and see if whoever's coming passes us, but if they see the hole, they won't just leave. It's now or never. Lincoln is practically dragging me now, but my leg won't let me move any faster. I'd tell him to leave me, but it wouldn't do any good, and might give away our position. So, I hobble as fast as I can, trying not to scream with each breath as the pain gets worse with every step. The shouts are so loud now, they must be right behind us.

We'll never outrun them. *Go, Lincoln, go.* But I don't have enough breath left to say the words aloud.

Come on, almost there. You got this.

Liv?

It's right there, but my leg is giving out. I feel a shove in my back and I'm falling....

CHAPTER 29

Excerpt Personal Diary: Dr. Ahmed Mahadow
Monday, February 19th, 2029
I'm not sure what has happened, but we were able to
flee after a police raid on the laboratory. We're headed
back to Rubezikan now with a police scientist who may
be able to help us. I hope it's not too late.

It's never the fall that kills you. It's the
landing. I tumble through the hole in the wall and land in a
messy heap on the other side. Everything hurts. Even if they
haven't remanned the wall with guards, I'll never make it to the
rendezvous point. *Where's Lincoln?* He was right next to me. *Oh
god. Didn't he make it?* I scramble to right myself and feel strong
arms under my shoulders. *Oh, thank god.*

"Jesus, Harbinger, we were just about to give up on you."

I lift my aching head and Casilla is there. I blink because I
must be hallucinating, but he's still there. Over his shoulder, I
spot Lincoln. I turn my head and find it's Jones helping me
stand.

"Hardja?" Casilla's voice is low and gruff.

I shake my head.

Casilla's face stiffens, but he nods "Let's go."

Gunfire on the other side of the wall focuses me. "I don't think I can walk," I hiss.

Casilla ignores me and motions Lincoln forward.

Then Jones lifts me up and deposits me in the back of an ATV next to Manganaro, who moans quietly and doesn't open his eyes. He doesn't look good. Shifting, I spy Valcross at the wheel. *Wait.*

"Where's Onai?"

Jones shakes his head as he gets Lincoln and Casilla into the back with me.

Oh.

Valcross starts the engine. It's surprisingly quiet. We're moving, weaving a path around buried mines, when my insides turn to water. I wait until we are well away from Yedys's wall, then lean in close to Jones so Lincoln won't hear. "Has anyone heard from Ben?"

Jones shakes his head.

Lincoln eyes me. "Mom, what is it?"

My throat closes up and I shake my head.

He inches closer. "What aren't you telling me?"

I wish the vehicle was making more noise now, but we're bumping over the sand with only a low purr. The motion is making the emptiness in my stomach churn and bile rises to the back of my throat.

Jones leans over to Lincoln. "She's worried about your dad, kid."

Lincoln's eyes go wide. "My dad?"

If I had more blood, if my hands were working, I'd throttle Jones.

"Mom, what does he mean? What's he talking about? Is Dad.... Was he at the lab, too?"

I can't speak, so I shake my head. *Oh please let Ben be okay.* Lincoln will blame himself. I want to send Liv out to find him, but a can barely feel her. We're both tapped. But it's almost over now. We'll get Ben and—

"Fuck me."

We slow, and I pull myself up onto my elbows. It's still dark, but there's a glowing orange light ahead. Something's on fire. *Oh, no. No, no, no.* Jones is jumping out with his night-vision goggles pulled down.

Casilla yells to him, "Do you see anything?"

"Two bodies. No heat sigs up."

It's the truck. Or what's left of the truck. It's been blown up and it's on fire. "Ben!"

I struggle to get off the ATV, but Casilla holds me back.

"Whoa, hang on. You might hurt yourself. Let Jones check. It might not be him."

"Let me go!" I shake out of Casilla's grasp, roll out of the back of the ATV, and fall onto the sand as my leg gives out. "Ben!" I'm crawling toward the bodies backlit by the flames when Lincoln gets an arm under my shoulder and scoops me up.

"We'll look together."

As we shuffle forward, I'm vaguely aware of Casilla cursing, but I couldn't care less. My mind flashes back to the lab at NYU and the bloody body I thought was Lincoln. But it wasn't. It wasn't him. It might not be Ben. *Can I let myself dare to hope?* We're close enough now that I drop down to my knees. The first body is on its stomach. Reaching out with damaged, trembling hands, I try to turn it over. When I can't, Lincoln leans down and gently pushes the body over. My heart stops mid-beat, but it's not Ben. I let out a breath that's a sob, holding back relief because there's another body to check and because he could still be in the blazing truck.

Before we reach the second body, Jones is kneeling next to it. "Not him."

I stare into the flames and chill runs through me. If Ben didn't get out of the truck in time.... *Ben, oh god.* Then a hand closes on my shoulder and someone pulls me back. I look up. It's Casilla. He's smiling. The fingers of my left hand clench as much as they're able and I deck him with my partial fist. White hot pain explodes from my hand and then I'm on the ground, breathing hard, and blinking up at Casilla's bloody nose.

"What the hell was that for?"

We left him in the truck so he would be safe. "Ben." My voice is rough as sandpaper.

"Harbinger, this is good. A good sign. He was supposed to blow up the truck if things got hot."

Jones comes up behind him. "I think I found tracks."

Casilla reaches down a hand. "Shall we go find your husband?"

———

TURNS OUT WE DON'T HAVE TO GO FAR. AS THE FIRST pink rays of morning peek out from between distant hills, Ben's outline emerges from the desert shadows. I want to leap out of the ATV and throw my arms around him, but all I can do is nod weakly as Lincoln jumps out and does it for me. The exhaustion and despair on Ben's face evaporate when he sees us. He slides a canvas bag off his shoulder and wraps his arms around Lincoln.

Oh my god, we did it. We're alive. I glance over at Manganaro's pale face and listen to his shallow, ragged breathing. *Well, most of us.*

As much as I want this moment of reunion to last, to hold the sweet joy of father and son reunited in my heart and mind, we need to get to safety. To a hospital, if possible. Casilla knows this, too.

"Get the fuck in the vehicle, Doc."

Ben nods. Wipes tears from his face, then picks up the bag. Lincoln helps him get it into the back as Ben hops on and Valcross takes off.

"What's in the bag?" Lincoln pokes it.

Ben leans down and kisses me softly on the cheek before replying. "It's a WHISP amplifier. I couldn't leave it behind in case it fell into the wrong hands." He smooths my hair. "So, what the hell happened? The last thing I saw was Casilla pointing a gun at Lincoln and then gunmen were approaching the truck and I had to blow it up."

I can grin now. "It's a long story."

Casilla comes out of the crumbling hut that passes for a hospital in the town I've already forgotten the name of. "Manganaro's gonna make it."

I let out a breath of air. "And you?"

"Oh, I'll be fine. Takes more than a couple of bullets to take me out. These weren't even hollow points, and I had one of the Rubezi scientists help me fish out the leg bullet while you and Lincoln were off saving the world."

A cough makes me wince as the Vicodin-dulled pain rears an angry head.

"You need to get in there next."

"No complaints here. I—"

Something is terribly wrong. My entire body goes taut, muscles screaming with tension, bullet holes expanding. *Could it be the virus taking hold?*

"Oh shit." Casilla is backing away. "Ben!"

I try to move, to turn my head, but the pain is terrible.

Something clamps around my throat and my air supply simply stops. Ben is here, his eyes wide with panic.

"My god, Sylvy, it's a WHISP! You have to fight it! You and Liv have to fight it! Hold on!" He runs toward the ATV.

Is he going to try to drive me away from it? *Liv are you there?* It's getting so dark. A cloud passes over the sun. But there aren't any clouds. The sky is clear and pale blue and stretches on forever.

CHAPTER 30

Recovered File CAW Server
Date: April 2, 2026
Particle to Particle Test 09: Subatomic
Exposure of subject's WHISP to a cumulative 1,000 mSv
over three days produced no noticeable changes in the
subject's WHISP, though the subject reported nausea.
Recommend an increase to 2,000 mSv plus or minus
added shielding of the human....

I'M SITTING AT LIV'S BEDSIDE. SHE DOESN'T LOOK
right. Parts of her are fuzzier than usual and she has spots
where she's missing pieces like an incomplete jigsaw puzzle.
Then someone's breathing draws my attention. It's Chester in
her wheelchair, staring with unseeing eyes. Terror floods my
veins. I grasp at Liv's hand but mine pass right through.

"Don't go, Liv! Don't leave me!"

Don't be afraid.

"But I could end up like her!"

Of me.

"What?"

The amplifier.

"I was afraid you'd go away and then get lost or hurt, and then I'd get hurt."

No. You were afraid of me. What would happen if I got stronger? Could you still control me?

"No, I...." My voice catches.

I'm you. I know it's true.

She's right. If I hadn't fought the amplifier maybe Liv could've done more. Maybe fewer people would have had to die, but I was afraid. I told myself it was fear of ending up like Chester, but Liv knew the truth all along. "I'm sorry."

Don't be sorry. Be brave.

"What?"

Because we're about to die. She lifts her hand and points behind me.

I turn my head and a WHISP is rushing toward us.

The world comes hurtling back and I'm on the ground gasping for breath. I blink and a blurry Ben comes into view holding something heavy and awkward. When he aims it at me, I recognize the amplifier. But won't it amplify the other WHISP, too?

Liv gives out and phantom hands encircle my throat again and squeeze. Images of Chester's victims parade through my head and I'm glad Casilla took away my cell phone at the start of the mission. Pleading, I reach out a mangled hand to Ben. *Hit me.*

This time, the buzz rattles deep in my bones and I'm flying apart, my molecules, my me, spreading out and out until I'm in between. Then, snap, I collapse back into myself, but I'm not myself, I'm Liv, and we're pissed. We grab the WHISP by its throat and yank it off me, but it elbows us and grips me again. *Oh no, you don't.* We reach for it again, but this time we go for where the eyes should be, digging in with shadow nails. Somewhere, someone screams. The WHISP abandons me and turns its full attention on us, crouching into a fighting stance.

Whoever owns this WHISP has had training in hand-to-hand combat. There are no weapons in its shadowy hands, and I'm drawn back to Chester and the sharp force trauma she produced with Ray. How did she do that?

The WHISP lunges and we dodge and roll then come up kicking. The kick misses, but the fact that we were able to kick at all thrills us. I glance down at our hands and clench and unclench both easily, marveling that we don't share my injuries. But we've gotten distracted and the WHISP is on me again. This time, it's trying to shove its hand into my mouth. We grab that arm and twist, applying pressure to the elbow. Somewhere, someone screams in agony and rage. But the WHISP throws us off and dives at me again, its arm seemingly uninjured. We groan in frustration and tackle it around the waist. Trying to pin it down, it snatches our wrist and snaps it, then rolls free.

Sylvia shrieks, but our wrist clicks back into place. This isn't going to work. The WHISP can hurt me through us and can kill me outright, but we can't stop it. Unless…. The WHISP goes for me again, but we manage to throw it off. *Hold him, Liv, I'll be right back.* And I'm Sylvia, and Lincoln is shouting at Ben, and I'm trying to get their attention.

"Ben!"

They both stop talking and look at me.

"Hit it with the amplifier. Make it disperse the particles instead of concentrate them."

Ben's pale face goes a shade paler. "But, I'll have to stop amplifying you"—he shakes his head—"Liv."

"We'll be fi—"

Invisible fingers close around my throat again and I have to go back to Liv. We're trying to pry the murderous WHISP's hands off Sylvia's throat.

Let go, I whisper soundlessly.

What? He'll kill us!

Ben's got this. I hope.

We drop away and everything shifts. I'm Sylvia, fighting for air, watching Liv's form shimmer. Is she growing dimmer or am I blacking out? A little of both? *Liv?* Ben. Lincoln. I love you…. Suddenly, my throat is open and hot, dry air rushes in. I'm on the ground gasping, wanting nothing more than to sleep for a week, but the killer WHISP might come back, might go after Lincoln.

"Ben." My voice is no more than a rasp. "Ben."

He's at my side. "I'm here, Baby, I'm here. We'll get you in the hospital. Can you stand?"

I can't shake my head, but I twitch. "No. Hit me again. Amplify us."

"What? Why?"

"Might"—a cough racks me, bringing blinding pain via my various battered and broken bones, but I need to make Ben understand—"come back."

Ben's whole face collapses in, but Lincoln is there too, now, and he nods.

"Get ready, Mom." He stands, but Ben clutches his leg.

"Lincoln! You could kill her!"

My stubbornness floods Lincoln's features. He points to his chest. "Then amplify me."

As pride floods my weary heart, it swells painfully in my chest. I can't let Ben send Lincoln's WHISP alone and I can't let this argument continue. It might already be too late to chase the WHISP. "Both!" My shout is so quiet, I'm not sure Ben or Lincoln even hears me. Breathing as deep as the pain allows, I try again. "Send us both. Ben, please. Send us both." Panting to catch my breath, I'm done talking. I hope Ben understands. *Please, Ben. Please.* The world is moving away now, down the long tunnel of unconsciousness. I fight to claw my way back, but I'm slipping.

Lincoln takes my numb hand. "Mom?"

He's so far away.

Then I'm Liv and we're flying across the desert, leaving the town and Sylvia and Ben and Lincoln behind us. Next to us Leo, Lincoln's WHISP, matches our speed. *Can I talk to him? Them?* But there's a truck just over the hill, not far, maybe a half a mile from the town. It's there, the killer WHISP, and its man. In fatigues, with guns and grenades, he looks like the men who took the virus. Another one of the ex-CIA? *Does it really matter?* His red face is both exhausted and furious. He's straining, trying to push his WHISP out, but it's too weak from the reversed amplifier hit.

"What the hell's wrong with you?" he screams.

Then Liv and I are on him. He can't see us in the sun, but his WHISP lunges at us. It has no face, but we swear we see a smirk as it thrusts a groping hand toward our stomach. Its fingers press in and pain like shards of glass pierces us. We feel something tremble within us. Something small and vulnerable. *My God. He's going for the baby.* It can't be true, but it is. We know it. Like falling through the icy surface of a lake, we're submerged in frigid horror. Then Leo is on the man's WHISP and yanking it back. Hot, venomous rage drives out the cold. We turn to the man.

We picture thrusting our ghost hand into his chest and squeezing his heart, feel our hands around his throat, then the com on his belt crackles to life, whining and hissing static. We don't have to envision it crammed down his throat, we've seen it many times. Our hand closes around it. *No!* I'm Sylvia on the ground on my back and someone's shining a light in my eyes. I turn my head as far as I'm able and vomit onto the sand. *Liv almost. I almost.* Liv is pulling me, but I can't go back. I was too close to doing the unthinkable. I spit, choke, spit again.

"West. Half mile. Over the hill. Hurry."

I think someone hears me. I think they will be okay, but then I remember the guns, the grenades. What if the man kills

Valcross or Casilla when I could have stopped him? *Stop him how?* If he was shooting at us and I had a gun, I wouldn't hesitate. He's trying to kill me and my unborn child. *Why can't I use Liv to protect myself? Why does it seem so wrong?* Then another thought smashes through my brain like a wrecking ball. *What if Lincoln uses Leo to kill him?* I have to get back.

CHAPTER 31

Patient Record: Rachel Chester
Date: January 28th, 2029
Although the patient remains in a catatonic state, Dr.
Sterhausch has prescribed a stringent regiment of stimu-
latory activities including providing the patient access to
a television three hours per day. Physical therapy to
prevent bedsores and muscle atrophy is ongoing, but the
need for armed supervision makes routine visits difficult
to schedule.

"Sᴙʟᴠʏ? Iᴍ ᴛᴜʀɴɪɴɢ ɪᴛ ᴏғғ!" Bᴇɴ's ᴋɴᴇᴇʟɪɴɢ
beside me.

No. I work my mouth, but no sound comes out. Clearing my
throat, I try again. "No. A little longer."

"But—"

I don't catch the rest of Ben's argument. I'm back with Liv.
Frustrated, we're trying to help Leo wrestle the killer WHISP,
but it's growing stronger. There must be some other way. The
man is getting in the truck. *Does he know Casilla and the others are
coming for him or is he just giving up?* He starts the engine. *How far*

can we follow him? Even with the amplifier, I'm not sure how much farther we can go. How far we'd dare to go. He's going to get away.

Then we spot it. A small, dark, too-square, gun-shaped device on his hip: a stun gun. *That's it.* We reach for it, but a force hauls us back. The man's WHISP has our ankle. *Where's Leo?* We kick and thrash, but abruptly the WHISP is like Superman and our limbs have gone cold and numb. We're drifting, the man and the truck fading. Ben must've turned off the amplifier. *Shit! No! We're so close!* The WHISP's hand loses its grip on our fading leg. With everything we have, we dive forward.

Zap!

"Clear!"

My body bucks on a hard, flat surface as pain rips through my chest. Then I'm coughing and sputtering and staring up into a too-bright light.

"Sylvy!" Ben's fingers close around my broken finger. I gasp and misinterpreting, he squeezes harder.

Moaning through gritted teeth, I utter two very important words, "Finger broken."

"Oh God! I'm sorry." He releases my hand.

The abrupt ceasing of pressure is almost as painful as his squeeze, but I try to smile.

"I'm just so glad…. I thought I'd lost you." His face is pale despite a fine coating of dust sticking to his sweat.

Grinning, Casilla appears by his side. "Mazel tov, by the way."

"What?" I'm distracted by someone fiddling with an I.V. in my arm, and it takes a moment to comprehend my surrounding. The room has the drab yellow walls and antiseptic smell of a hospital room, but the equipment I spot is dated and worn and there aren't any calming watercolor paintings.

"On your family's new addition."

His words sink in slowly as I study his face. *How could he possibly know?* I'm considering my response when Ben leans in and kisses my forehead.

"They did an ultrasound to check for internal bleeding."

"Ah."

Casilla's face turns serious. "There may be repercussions from the agency for not telling us about that."

"Why? It wasn't an issue."

He shakes his head. "It's an underlying medical condition. Could have compromised the mission."

"Okay, fine." I raise my eyebrows and widen my eyes. "What? I'm pregnant? I had no idea."

He gives me an incredulous look. "Nice try."

Ben cuts in. "Hey. The way I see it, she's the one who got the virus back from your crazy, terrorist pals, and stopped one of their most dangerous wonder soldiers. Without her, this mission would've been pretty much a complete failure. They should give her a goddam medal."

I could care less what the CIA thinks of me, but something Ben says hiccups in my head. "Wonder soldiers?"

Ben and Casilla exchange a dark look and Casilla walks away.

Smoothing my hair, Ben sighs. "Yeah. It turns out, the guy you stunned was part of a secret government project called the Wonder Soldier Program."

Wonder Soldier Program. Something about the way Ben says it gives me pause. Then I realize. "WSP. WHISP. You don't mean…"

Ben nods. "They made WHISPs, or, at least, the technology that makes WHISPs, and then that technology, a microchip, somehow got out into the public and bam, normal people have them, too."

This makes no sense. "But if they know what causes WHISPs, then why don't they just stop it?"

Ben shrugs. "It's not that simple. It's not really a thing, it's the way a lot of technology works now. They'd have to redo a ton of infrastructure and change manufacturing processes, but more importantly, the government would have to admit WHISPs are all their fault and that they were trying to use the technology to create super-soldiers. Not going to happen."

I can see why they'd want a WHISP virus, to stop "wonder" soldiers, but then, why test it publicly on civilians? Why release it into New York City? "Okay, but how does the Wonder Soldier Program lead to ex-CIA WHISP terrorists?"

"Casilla says it was a Pandora's Box situation. People involved in the program wanted to fix their mistakes and decided that killing WHISPers was the way to do it."

In addition to all my other aches and pains, my head is starting to hurt. I can't dwell on this now, so I let my eyes scan the room. "Where's Lincoln?"

"Sleeping. He was in pretty bad shape after the amplifier exploded."

"Yeah, I b—wait, what?"

Ben doesn't meet my eyes. "Yeah, turns out, it's not entirely stable. Especially when used for extended periods of time."

My eyes rake over him. "Are you okay?"

"Thankfully, I was by you and Lincoln at the time, and maybe exploded is a bit—"

Valcross slaps Ben on the back and Ben winces. "Took two big metal shards in back, but will live."

Ben's face is red. "You might not if you don't stop slapping my back."

Valcross shrugs and lifts a bandaged leg. "Kick shin, if you want."

Ben rolls his eyes.

I grin, but it fades as I remember that we didn't all make it out. I turn my head toward Valcross. "Did Hardja and Onai have families?"

Valcross frowns. "I don't know."

"But you've gone on missions with them before, right?"

"Da. We don't talk about family. Bad for mission." He lifts his chin. "Is sad, but sadder if thousands die from virus, da?"

Reluctantly, I nod.

"Cheer up. Transportation should be here in few hours. You and your family," he gestures to my stomach, "should be home in two days."

Home. I picture Ben and Lincoln nestled on Lincoln's miniature couch, Grumps the Cat trying to find a space between them. My eyelids flutter closed, but then snap open.

"What will you do with the wonder soldier? How are you containing his WHISP? A Faraday cage?"

Valcross glances away and clears his throat. "You should rest now."

I look to Ben. "Did you rig something up for them?"

Ben's face has gone stiff. "They didn't ask me to, no."

He doesn't have to say more. The truth is all over his face. They killed him. A righteous anger crests within me, but then recedes. *Did I really think they were going to risk transporting him back to America for trial?* I may have kidded myself about it, may not have been willing to pull the trigger myself, but deep down, I knew.

"Oh."

Ben gazes into my eyes. His are conflicted. "We were going to blow up a whole lab full of innocent scientists."

"We thought they were terrorists." But he has a point. Still, the wonder soldier's death doesn't sit right. He'd been neutralized, wasn't an immediate threat, and didn't have the virus. I don't like this greater good justice. I'm glad we're going home.

He reaches out to stroke my face. "I love you."

"We know." The words are out of my mouth before my mouth checks in with my brain.

"We?"

I open my mouth to respond, but someone kicks down the door and the room fills with armed soldiers.

CHAPTER 32

Encrypted CIA Internal Communication (partial)
…with disastrous results…immediately terminated and
all trace of the WSP program eradicated per protocol
Black Hole.

I REACH FOR MY GUN BUT, OF COURSE, IT ISN'T
there. Ben grips my hand and pain rushes through my broken
finger again, but it's distant compared to the sharp fear and
bitter taste of metal coating my tongue. My eyes find Ben's
then Lincoln's. If this is the end, I want my last sight to be of
my family. Holding my breath, I brace myself, but there's no
barrage of gunfire, only the barking of orders I don't understand. Then the soldiers grab Ben, put a bag over his head, and
drag him away. As his fingers slip from my awkward grip, I
reach for him.

"Ben!"

A soldier shouts at me and points his rifle at my face. Then
everything goes dark, hot, and stifling and I'm being roughly
lifted and set on my feet. My legs support me, but just barely.
More shouting erupts, this time with a distinct edge of fear, and
the hands holding me release. I wobble and resist the urge to

pluck the bag from my head. The number of voices increases. *Is one of them Casilla's?* As the room grows quiet, the unmistakable click of a gun being cocked echoes next to my ear. Instinct tells me to hold very still. Maybe I could reach out with Liv and "see" what's going on, but something in my gut tells me that's a bad idea. Someone speaks, I think in Rubezi, slowly, softly, calmly. Close to me comes an angry reply. Then something cold and hard hits the back of my head.

———

MY HEAD IS ACHING, AND THE WORLD IS SPINNING IN slow, nauseating circles, but I'm alive. I reach out for Liv, but she's still MIA. *Could it be the virus? How long has it been? How long did it take Isabel to show signs? A couple of days? What about Lincoln? Without Liv, I can't know if either of us is infected. If he's still alive. The men, the guns....* As I rise from the depths of unconsciousness, Ben's voice sets my heart thumping. He's alive, too. I stir my heavy eyelids and eventually manage to lift them. The light is brighter than I'd expect for a prison camp, and the bunk more comfortable, too. But no, we're not in a cell, we're in a room, and I'm lying on a couch.

"Sylvy!" Ben kneels next to me and touches my face. "Baby, can you hear me?"

"Where are we?" My voice is like dry leaves rustling.

"Lincoln, get your mom some water."

Lincoln, thank God. I push myself up and the room tilts like a carnival ride. Breathing deep to avoid vomiting, I close my eyes. Soon something cool and wet is pressed against my forehead.

"Can you drink?"

Nodding without opening my eyes, a glass nudges my lips and I sip the cold water within. The nausea recedes enough to ask, "What's going on?"

Ben clears his throat. "We're not exactly sure, but Casilla thinks we're in the palace."

"Palace?"

"In Tarbygan."

"Oh. Okay." I understand the words, but they make no sense. Ben puts the glass to my lips again and I drink.

"Are you hungry?"

I shake my head and wait for the nausea to return. When it doesn't, I open my eyes. Ben's face is drawn with worry but relaxes a little when I look at him. I crook a corner of my mouth and he kisses my forehead. When he draws back, I take in the rest of the room. It's larger than I first thought, and much more opulent. The floor is marble, and I think the walls are, too. Huge windows along one wall are adorned with floor-length, golden curtains, and most of the numerous couches, including the one I'm sitting on, have velvety, gold cushions.

Casilla, Jones, and Valcross are conversing in low tones not far away, but I don't spot Manganaro anywhere, which causes a small empty hole to form in my chest. Lincoln's hovering just behind Ben. I motion him closer. "Hey, how are you?"

When he's nearer, the red of his eyes is more noticeable. "A little woozy, but I'll be okay."

"Woozy?"

Ben cuts in, "They hit him with a tranquilizer dart. He's only been awake a little longer than you."

Reaching back with my right hand, which I'm relieved to find I'm able to feel and clench into a fist again, I gently finger the lump on the back of my skull. "Wish they would've darted me, too. Why—?" But before Ben answers, it comes to me. "Our WHISPs."

Ben nods. "We think so."

I bring my hand away from my head, but the throb my touch initiated remains. "So, why are we here as opposed to...."

"Dead?" Lincoln offers.

Ben grimaces. "Casilla's not sure. But he's hopeful."

"I don't see Manganaro. Did he—?" My throat tightens.

Ben glances away. "I'm not sure. He wasn't here when they took the bags off our heads."

"They didn't tell you anything?"

"Casilla said they told us to wait here." Ben looks around, then points to a nearby table. "I think it's a good sign that they left us water and little sandwiches, though."

At the mention of sandwiches, my stomach is caught in that terrible place between hunger and nausea, but I know I haven't eaten in hours, maybe a whole day. I touch Lincoln's arm. "Can you get me a sandwich, please?"

He nods and turns, but then turns back to me. "Mom?"

"Yeah?"

His face is hard to read. "Are you really pregnant?"

I chuckle. The entire situation is so surreal I worry for a moment that I might still be unconscious and dreaming, but my face flushes, nonetheless. "Yeah. I am."

His wonder is tinged with an expression I can only describe as "ewww" as his mouth works to form words. "Oh. Wow." He turns again and walks over to the table with the refreshments.

I lean closer to Ben. "How's he holding up?"

Ben smiles without much joy. "Good. Maybe better than me. He's a good kid. We did a good job." He stops abruptly and the smile fades. What he's not saying is he hopes he'll get the chance to be a good man.

Lincoln comes back with several sandwiches on a small china plate with intricate gold trim. I smile at him and take one. Shifting my position, I'm reminded of all the injuries I've sustained in the past few days and wonder if we could ask for ibuprofen. As I nibble on the sandwich, I try to catch Casilla's attention, but he seems to be avoiding my gaze. He looks quite good for a man shot three times. I guess he's used to it. Lincoln sets the plate down on a low table next to the couch, and I turn to Ben.

"You said Casilla was hopeful. What did you mean?"

Ben chews the insides of his cheeks before answering. "Well, he said there were only two reasons they would take us to Tarbygan. One is that the president is going to negotiate our release with the CIA in exchange for either money or favors." He hesitates.

I pop the rest of the small sandwich into my mouth, chew, and swallow before asking, "And the second?"

Ben clears his throat and doesn't meet my eye. "With Yedys compromised, Tarbygan is the most secure place in Rubezikan." He stops, but I know that isn't all. Especially when he shoots Lincoln a warning look.

"Ben."

"It's a good place for making a public demonstration."

Pieces fall into place. The sandwich churns in my belly and threatens to reappear. "And by demonstration, you mean execution."

"Casilla didn't say that."

"No, of course not." No need to panic us. My mind flies into overdrive. *Are there any ventilation ducts? Do the windows have bars? Is there more than one door to the room? What can I use as a weapon?* I stand, but my leg gives out and I slump against Ben as he catches me.

"Sylvy, whoa, what are you….?"

Casilla finally shambles over. "Easy. I know what you're thinking, Harbinger, but take a good look around." He points up between two chandeliers at a high-tech camera like the ones in casinos. "We're pretty screwed."

His casual tone gets my hackles up, but I sit so as not to look too suspicious and shield my mouth with my hand. "Surely, you have some kind of plan."

He lets his gaze wander around the room, to the other agents, to Ben, to Lincoln, and then finally back to me. His face is sober, grim, and he doesn't bother to hide what he's saying from the camera. "Sorry. This is what we in the business call an 'end scenario'."

Encrypted Communication President Alperen Pargulmahamadomet: CIA
What the hell do you think you are doing? My scientists
said you imprisoned them and created a virus to kill my
people. This is an act of war.
Highest and Most Honorable, Venerable, and
Worshipped President Alperen Pargulmahamadomet

MY BLOOD TURNS TO ICE. THIS CAN'T BE RIGHT. WE
got Lincoln back. We escaped. We beat the bad guys. I drop my
hand into my lap. "But you said you were hopeful."

He gives me a sad, what-would-you-have-said look.

I'm grasping now. "Surely, we can explain the misunderstanding. Tell them we thought they'd kidnapped my son."
But the excuse sounds ridiculous and I know it. *So sorry we
attacked and invaded your prison camp. We'll certainly donate to the
families of all the guards we killed. We swear we're the good CIA guys,
not the bad ones. Fuck.* But maybe. "What about the scientists?
Wouldn't they be able to explain what really happened? Vouch
for us?"

"If the facility survived?" Casilla pauses. "Maybe."

"What do you mean, 'If the facility survived?' We didn't blow up the lab, did we?"

"No." He sighs. "But we weren't the only ones there, were we?"

I sink back into the soft cushions. "But you checked before you left, right? Made sure they didn't...." The look on his face silences me.

Lincoln and Ben join me on the couch and we huddle together as a family. Maybe for the last time.

"Mom, I'm—"

I grab Lincoln's hand. "No. This isn't your fault. Not even a little."

"But I could've tried to get the scientists to send a message to the American embassy. I could've done something to let you know what was going on, that I was okay. I just didn't think it through. I wanted to help them, and I didn't know who to trust, and—"

"It's okay." I stop myself from saying it's going to be okay. I don't know that, don't really feel that.

Ben's hand and eyes find mine, giving me a well-at-least-we're-together squeeze and look. The door bursts open and the reassuring pressure becomes painful as impeccably dressed soldiers march in and surround us. My gaze shoots to Casilla, but he's watching the soldiers, his stance a little too relaxed. A few of the soldiers stride over to the couch and prod us to stand with the butts of their rifles. With Lincoln and Ben supporting me, I manage it. Finally, a soldier with a large, white feather in his cap and a baton a little longer than a drum major's comes through a gap in the ranks that folds in around him. He motions curtly with one white-gloved hand.

"Come."

Casilla turns to me and gives a slight nod, though I'm not exactly sure why. Not following the soldiers really doesn't seem like any kind of an option, at this point. Briefly, I consider faking passing out, but that might only get me separated from Ben and Lincoln, pretty much the opposite of what I want right now. So, we hobble out wedged between CIA agents, Casilla in the front and Jones and Valcross in back. The surrounding soldiers stare straight ahead as we pass down a wide marble hallway with enormous paintings of the same man hung in gilded frames. The president of Rubezikan, no doubt. The godlike renderings don't give me much hope of a rational discussion with him.

The head soldier stops at a floor-to-ceiling door of what looks like pure gold and our whole procession comes to a halt. He knocks three times with a huge door knocker and a few seconds later, the doors part and open inward. Golden light spills into the hallway from the room beyond. The room is blinding and beautiful and terrifying all at the same time. Our judge, jury, and executioner waits inside that room for us. That it's one of the most gorgeous rooms I've ever seen, makes the fact we might be about to die that much more surreal.

The room itself is grand simply in size. I have to crane my neck to see the behemoth, bejeweled chandeliers above. The floor is still white marble, but now inlaid with spiraling patterns of gold. From the walls, intricate carvings depict scenes of gods and monsters. I almost expect a throne, but instead there is an enormous desk with a white marble top. At the throne-like chair behind the desk is a rather short man with smooth, tan skin, bushy black eyebrows over pale brown eyes, and a mat of thick, black hair, wearing an impeccable black suit with a light gray patterned tie. President Pargulmahamadomet is not what I expected from a ruthless dictator, but my cop spider senses are tingling. It's always the non-assuming ones you have to be wary of.

The president doesn't look up from a computer integrated into the surface of his desk until the head soldier with the feather stands before his desk and thumps the butt of his baton on the floor three times. Glancing up as if he's just noticed the squad of soldiers and small cadre of prisoners before him, the president nods to the soldier then looks the six of us up and down, his gaze lingering rather longer on Lincoln and me. When he speaks, it's with an air of easy authority. "You folks have had a busy few days, yes?"

From the way he says folks, I get the feeling he doesn't say the word very often, that he's using a quaint American term for our benefit.

Silence stretches for almost half a minute before he finally sighs. "You may speak."

Casilla clears his throat. "Thank you, Mr. President. You're most gracious—"

The president cuts him off with a wave of his hand. "Yes, yes, I'm a great man. Skip to Yedys." His eyes blaze into Casilla.

"A terrible misunderstanding, Mr. President."

The president nods gravely. "Yes, misunderstanding, yes. Americans understand all people like me to be terrorists, no? Have brown skin, must be terrorist, must blow them up." He thumps a fist down on his desk. "I am right, yes?"

Casilla has the good sense to look miserable. "I can see how it might look that way, Sir."

Regarding the surface of his desk, the president sighs again. "CIA, CIA, what to do with you? So many choices. Cut off your heads in front of the Great Monument of Rubezikan Independence, throw you in the presidential dungeons, try to trade you back to your country for cash"—he looks up brightly —"or trade you to some other country for cash. Yes, even better."

I'm not certain there's an opportune time for me to cut in, but I feel now is as good a time as any. "We're not CIA." I motion to myself, Ben, and Lincoln.

"Of course not!" the president snaps. "I know this. You are tainted cop and scientist and scientist's tainted son." He looks us over more carefully, eyes hooded. "I send you back to Yedys, I think."

My mind goes to a dark, underground cell with Lincoln sitting on a cot with a threadbare sheet, his face gaunt and hopeless. Then another flash. A baby being taken from my arms as I scream and thrash; Liv reaching her shadowy arms out and meeting an invisible wall. My heart grinds painfully in my chest, then stops. The room darkens, spins away. But then a memory sparks and kindles into a flame of remembrance: men and women in dim cells and the bad CIA agent flinging the WHISP virus into my face and into the faces of the nearest prisoners, of his boot crushing the vial, of the sprinklers washing the virus along the corridor into other cells. My bargaining chip.

"They're all going to die," my voice is so hollow, it doesn't seem to be coming from my throat, rather from somewhere deeper.

"What? What did you say?" the president's rage echoes in the cavernous room. The soldier nearest to me winces, his fingers tightening around his rifle.

"The WHISPers in Yedys. The bad CIA agents released the virus into the cellblocks. They only have a few days to live unless...."

His scleras bulge with too much white and froth spits from his lips. "Unless what?"

"She knows how to cure it. She's done it before," Casilla chimes in with a steady, calm voice devoid of pleading or threat and full of promise.

The president stands and smacks his desk with an open palm then points first to me, then Casilla. "You lie! You all lie! You poisoned my people! I'll have all of your heads!"

"Please, Sir! Please, ask the prisoners! Ask the scientists!" Lincoln begs.

"Don't tell me—"

The president whips around to face Lincoln and point a trembling finger at him. Just then, blue smoke billows up from the president's back. As the smoke dims the bright sunlight, I glimpse a faint but unmistakable outline. President Pargulma-hamadomet has a WHISP.

CHAPTER 34

Encrypted Communication: President Alperen Pargulmahamadomet
Dear Most Honorable President Pargulmahamadomet:
There has been a grave misunderstanding. The CIA
knows of no such person [Martin Exavier Ruftin], and
we have no such office [CIA Executive Director of
WHISP Affairs]. We have no knowledge of an engineered
virus meant for the extermination of any populous. It
does not benefit us to begin an international event at
this time.
Sincerely,
Bolton Ridley McMahonnon, Director of the Central
Intelligence Agency

MY EYES FLIT TO LINCOLN, AND THOUGH HIS FACE IS
a mask, I can see it in his eyes. He did something with Leo, like
he did in Yedys with the sprinklers. A mad laugh bubbles up to
the back of my throat but I swallow it down. The president
must've been wearing some kind of device to mask his WHISP,
like a WHISP generator, but opposite. Now I have a real

bargaining chip. He may not care enough to save his people, but he sure as shit cares about himself. How to spin it?

The president doesn't glance over his shoulder. He can see our eyes on his WHISP. The crimson of embarrassment is quickly replaced by beet red rage. He'll kill us all for having seen his WHISP. I have to act fast.

"Oh no. Mr. President, Sir, I'm so sorry. I didn't know. I didn't mean to...."

"Didn't mean to what?" he screams.

Lincoln catches on, thank god. My smart boy.

"She's been infected with the virus"—Lincoln takes a breath —"by the others. I think we both have."

"Get them out! Kill them!" the president shrieks, pointing at our group.

The soldiers close in around us. Strong hands grasp my shoulders, my arms. *Fuck.* "It's too late! You've already been exposed. I'm the only one who's ever cured the virus, the only one who knows how, the only one who can, but I need their help. Only they can make the machines to help me." I reach for Ben and Lincoln with this last white lie. I don't mean to throw Casilla and the others under the bus, but I can't think of a reason I'd need them, too. Hopefully, I'll be able to negotiate for their lives, just not right now. Right now, I need President Pargulmahamadomet to bite down on the hook of his only chance of survival. Realistically, he probably isn't close enough to be exposed, even if I have contracted the virus this time. I glance at Lincoln, grunting and struggling with his own soldiers, hoping that a natural immunity runs in our family. I've cured the virus before, but Liv's weak right now, and I've no idea if I can cure it again. Maybe Ben and Lincoln could work with the Rubezi scientists to make the machine that almost killed me actually work.

Provided the lab wasn't completely destroyed.

My thoughts run wild as we're being dragged from the room. *Please. Please.*

"Wait!"

Everything stops. I sag in my captors' grips. *Please.*

The president's stare is cold but calculating. He isn't an idiot. He still holds all the cards. He could force us to cure the virus and then murder us all. "How do I know you're not lying? How do I know there even is a virus?"

I almost tell him about Ben's tests, but I stop myself. It didn't really work for me, and if he tests the president and there are no abnormalities, the president may think we were lying and have us killed on the spot. "There's no way to know until the end, until the WHISP is sick enough that the person starts dying."

"We'll see. Bring the scientists!"

The head soldier barks orders in Rubezi and about twenty soldiers break off from the back of the room and scurry out. The president then growls something to the head soldier and they both retreat behind a screen to the left of the desk, probably to remove the faulty device from under the President's clothing. The seconds tick by, each one an eternity. I want to touch Ben, to hug Lincoln, but the soldiers have us separated by more than an arm's length. Suddenly, it occurs to me that I should be thrilled there are scientists to retrieve. It means the lab wasn't destroyed. There's still hope. Crisp and dapper, the president returns in a new suit, this one a deep navy. He must've also replaced the concealing device because his WHISP has vanished. Poised once again, the president takes a seat at his desk. Without being told, the head soldier pours him a drink from a crystal decanter on a stand behind the desk and sets it within the president's reach.

Beginning to wonder if the soldiers are marching all the way to Yedys to collect the scientists, my vision blurs and the room spins.

"Sylvy!"

"Mom?"

"What is wrong with her? Is it the virus?" The president can't mask his anxiety.

I'm on the floor and the soldiers who were holding me up are now pointing their guns at me with drawn faces and trembling hands. I'd tell them that the virus only affects WHISPers, but I'm not sure they speak English.

"She's just weak. She was injured," Ben's voice is strained, probably from struggling to get to me.

"Could that accelerate the virus?" Now there's real terror lacing the president's words.

Could it? I close my eyes and reach out to Liv, but it's almost like she's sleeping. *Liv?* A stirring, but no answer. I think we're fine, just tired; still, knowing I can't rely on her right now sends a shiver down my spine.

"Sylvy?"

I haven't answered Ben. Opening my eyes, I turn my head toward his voice. "I'm okay." *Maybe.*

It's then that the soldiers return with the scientists. From my vantage point on the floor, I can't see how many they've brought with them or which ones. Hopefully, friends of Lincoln, though I'm not sure how far they will go to protect him in front of their president. The soldiers surrounding us shift as the scientists are brought closer to the president, and Ben's foot is close enough to touch now, though I dare not move at this critical point. He's handsome in his dirty fatigues and combat boots; not soldier handsome, but scientist-thrust-into-warzone handsome. I hope there's a later opportunity to tell him so.

The president barks something in Rubezi. Casilla would understand, but I can't see him among the trees of military legs. In a voice like a kicked puppy, one of the scientists responds. The president replies, his words clipped. I should've at least listened to a how-to-speak-Rubezi CD or gotten an app for my phone. My concentration on the conversation lags. Rationally, I know it's very important to me. The outcome is life or death, after all, but not being able to understand makes listening so very tiring. I'm drifting off when the pain comes.

At first, I think the president has decided we're lying and to kill us all, and that I've been shot in the abdomen. Pain sharp as knives cuts through my pelvis. *Why not aim for the head? Is this the start of a long series of tortures? Oh god, do they know about the baby?* The pain crescendos then begins to fade. *Am I going into shock?* I open my eyes, but nothing seems to have changed. I strain to look at my own naval, but there's no wound. *What the—*

The pain, ebbed to nothing, starts again.

I cry out. Guns swivel and point at me. Something's wrong. Has the stress pushed me into labor? *Oh please no.* I look to Ben for comfort, but the color has drained from his face.

"Please, please let me go to her," his words are soft and pleading.

Another burst of pain wracks me. *Liv!* She wakes and presses a cool, gray hand over my eyes. *Sleep.* The pain eases, and everything goes dark.

———

I WAKE TO ECHOES OF PAIN IN MY ABDOMEN. *DID I LOSE the baby?* My heart stutters as the selfishness of my reckless behavior crashes down on me. It's hard to breathe.

"Mom?"

Lincoln? I open my eyes and my son stares back at me. At least, I saved Lincoln. I lift a hand to touch his face, but find my arm is strapped down. *Or did I?* My heart speeds to a gallop as I move my other arm and find it also restrained. "What's going on? Where's your dad?"

Lincoln rests a hand on my forehead. "It's okay. He's okay. I can probably unstrap you soon. They just wanted to make sure you weren't trying something."

I search his face. He's holding back. "What else? Did I—" I swallow hard and drop my voice to a whisper, "Did I lose the baby?"

"What? No. No. It was false labor."

Light-headed with relief, I sink back into the pillow, but then remember where we are. "What happened with the president and the scientists? Is Casilla—" I have to stop and catch my breath.

"Okay, so things were pretty bad for a while, especially after you passed out. The president was sure you were trying to pull something on him and then he thought you were dying of the virus, and then Dr. Abdullayev told him you hadn't been lying about the virus and that several vials were missing. He finally let a doctor examine you, and then, well,,,." Lincoln gestures around.

"So, President Pargulmahamadomet knows I'm pregnant?"

Lincoln cringes and nods. "Is that bad?"

I try to keep the fear from my voice. "Maybe. It gives him more things to threaten us with." *Me with.*

"Mom?"

"Yeah."

"Can you check me for the virus?"

I bolt as upright as the restraints allow. "Why? Do you feel sick?"

"No. I just...want to make sure."

I reach out to Liv. She feels stronger, but I'm still not sure we're up for the task. Gently, I guide her closer to Lincoln, and closer to Leo. Probing, I let myself look through Liv's eyes, but Leo's clean. We reach out and place a hand on his shoulder. No images of sticky, putrid blackness or inky, crawling legs assault us. Then I'm back to me.

"You're good." Maybe we do have some kind of immunity. Lincoln lets out a breath.

I should've checked him before. He's been worried.

"Maybe you can teach me."

"Teach you what?"

Lincoln gives me a "duh" look. "How to cure the virus."

I picture Lincoln in the cellblock again, surrounded by dying WHISPers. "No."

His lower lip juts out stubbornly. "There are a lot of exposed people. You can't check them all by yourself. I can help."

"Lincoln, I—" Scuttling at the edges of my vision. *Liv?* I reach out, but my thought gets caught in tar. Darkness oozes toward me. I yank myself back to myself. *Oh no.*

CHAPTER 35

www.forbiddenknowledge.com

Post September 29th, 2027: WHISPs
Proof the government knew about WHISPs and what
causes them is all around us. Help me unleash it by
signing my petition for the release of CIA documents
under the Freedom of Information Act.

"SHIT."

Lincoln's face is ashen. "Mom, what's wrong? Is it the baby again?"

"No, no. I, um...I think...maybe...." The words stick in my throat. *Could I still infect Lincoln? What if the virus mutates or something?* "Can you go get your dad for me?"

Suspicion clouds Lincoln's eyes.

"Please?"

"I think so. It might take a little while."

"That's okay. It's not like I'm going anywhere." I shift a strapped arm for effect.

His eyebrows knit.

I shouldn't have tried humor. Lincoln knows me too well.

"Mom, I—"

"Please, Lincoln."

"Okay. But I'll be back as soon as I can."

He turns, walks to one of the doctors or scientists or whoever is on the other side of the room and speaks to them in a low voice I can't make out. Then he turns back and waves to me before going out the door. The man walks over to my bed.

"Lincoln wants me to take off the strapping. If I do this and you run away, it will be bad for all of us, but me and him, especially. Do you understand?" Though weighted by a Rubezi accent, his English is pretty good.

"Yes. Thank you. But you can't let Lincoln back in here."

The man's face twists in confusion. "Why?"

"I'm infected."

He'd reached for the strap on my right arm; he now pulls back. The confusion turns to something more like fear. His gaze drops to the side of the bed, like he's trying to peer underneath. "But...but Lincoln said you are immune, that you cure virus. You said—"

"I have cured the virus before, but I wasn't infected then. I...I don't think I can do it now." I want to reach out to Liv again, to see if I can get past it to her, but I'm afraid I won't be able to, afraid I'll do more harm than good.

His fear degrades into despair. "But if you can't cure it, then what about Yedys?"

How many WHISPers were there? Fifty? A hundred? Could I have really cured them all on my own? "There might be another way."

"Another way?"

"That's why I need to speak to my husband. He's a scientist, too. But you can't let Lincoln back in. Not yet. Not until I'm sure." Involuntarily, I strain against the straps. Claustrophobic panic touches my chest, and I lean back and take in a shaking breath. "Also, can you please unstrap me?"

———

"Sylvy, I—"

"Ben, I love you, too, but we really don't have time for this." Actually, I've no idea how much time I have. It was a few days before Isabel died, but if this virus is mutated or stronger....

Focus.

"I need you and Lincoln to make the machine you tried to use to cure the virus."

Ben's gray face pales a shade. "Sylvy, it almost killed you last time."

"I know, but I have an idea about how to fix it." *Maybe.*

"But I don't have a lab or any equipment."

"Work with the scientists here. I'm sure they have something similar, and maybe you can salvage some components from the amplifier."

In holding back his fear, Ben's doubt seeps through into his face and his voice, "Are you sure you can't cure it the way you did for those other people?"

I take a deep breath. "No, but I'm afraid to try to reach out to Liv again. It's blocking me, and I could make things worse."

Ben nods. "Okay. Okay. But I don't like leaving you here." Ben glances around the bare hospital room. "What if the president changes his mind?"

I almost say 'He won't,' but I can't. It's a lie, and one too flimsy to hold. "The faster you work, the less time he'll have to change it."

Cupping my head in his hands, Ben nestles his forehead against mine. "I can't lose you."

"I trust you. You can do this." I kiss his trembling lips.

He kisses back, gently at first, then fiercely.

I want to reciprocate, but instead I pull away. "Now go. And tell our son that I love him."

Ben lets me go and stands. "You can tell him yourself when this is done."

He turns and leaves the room without looking back. I'm glad. I don't want him to see the tears in my eyes. I touch the indent on the bedsheet where he was sitting. It's still warm. Now, I just have to figure out how to make his machine work.

————

SHOCKINGLY, MY REQUEST FOR SOME OF THE scientists' notes on the virus is granted, but my joy is soon crushed. The notes are, of course, in Rubezi. I glance around the room and find it empty for the first time. I hadn't noticed the exodus of doctors and guards after the notes were delivered. *Dammit.* I get up. The tile floor is like ice on my bare feet, and I'm more lightheaded than I want to be. I steady myself using the bed for support and then glance behind me at Liv. She looks the same as always, not thinner or droopy or spread out like I thought she might, and she shadows my movements like nothing's wrong. Yet, I can feel a resistance, like a hand dragging through water. *Focus.* Turning away, I gingerly head for the door. To my surprise, it opens with little effort, but two guards on the opposite side raise their rifles at me when it does. I hold up my free hand.

"Whoa, I just need an interpreter."

They stare and don't lower their guns.

"For the notes? English?" I point to one of them and then the other and then to my own mouth. "Rubezi?"

The slightly shorter guard says something in Rubezi. I'm encouraged since it sounds more like a question than a command.

"Right, yes." I point to my mouth again. "I need an interpreter."

The shorter soldier nods and then motions me back into the room with his rifle.

"Okay, but if you could hurry."

Now he says something more commanding and gestures more emphatically with the rifle.

"Fine. Thank you."

I retreat behind the closed door and lean against it, gathering my strength for the trip back to the bed. A bitter gnawing of fear grows in my stomach. The room isn't that big. I shouldn't need to rest. *Is it the virus?* I take a deep breath. *No, you idiot, it's probably the false labor and fifteen other injuries you suffered in the past two days. Two days? Three days?* I glance around the room, but there are no clocks or windows. The small part of me that wants to search for anything useful as a weapon is squashed when I spot the video camera in the ceiling. So much for that idea, or for escaping through the ductwork like in a spy movie. Limping back to the bed, I wonder how long it will take for the guards to summon someone. The knock at the door comes just after I've thrown the thin blanket over my bandaged and scarred legs. The words "Come in" are on the tip of my tongue when the door opens and a man in scrubs rolls in a cart with a tray of food on it. *Shit.*

"You don't speak English, do you?"

The man smiles at me vaguely as he rolls the cart closer. When I don't move, he brings his hands up to his mouth and gestures eating then rubs his belly and makes an mmmm sound.

I sigh and then nod. "Yeah, thanks."

He turns to go.

"Wait!"

He turns back and I grab some of the note pages and point to them.

"I need help with these." I mime reading them, then shake

my head frowning and shrug my shoulders in my best I-don't-get-it way.

He stares blankly back at me.

Frustration bubbles up and makes me want to throw the tray of food, but I'm certain that would just get me restrained again, so instead I grab his arm. "Please. I need English. Eeenglish." I make the fingers of my other hand into a "V" and point at his eyes with them, then at the papers, then at his mouth, then at my ear. "You read. You tell me what says."

His gaze flies up to the camera and then down to my hand on his arm. Shaking his head, his face goes red and beads of moisture appear on his forehead. He pulls away and nearly runs from the room. I throw my hands up in defeat then rub my temples. *Why is this so hard?* Anger boils in my stomach. Snatching up some of the notes, I swing my legs over to the edge of the bed and wave the pages up at the camera.

"I need a translator! A translator! A trans-lat—"

"You don't have to shout."

CHAPTER 36

Archive: Department of Defense 1955: Death Frequency
The conclusion of our research at this time is there is no
known frequency of sound waves that will result in the
death of a mammal. Further research into the lethality of
more focused ultrasonic and infrasonic waves is needed.

CASILLA'S WRISTS ARE CUFFED BEHIND HIS BACK AND
he's accompanied by two soldiers, different from the ones
outside my door. There are fresh wounds on his face and one of
his eyes is swollen shut, but he's alive. I hadn't been sure until
now. I have to take in a deep breath to keep from sobbing with
relief. "You look terrible."

"Have you looked in the mirror lately? Pot, kettle...."

"How're...." No time and may not want to know. "I need
your help with these." I motion to the pile of papers on the
stand next to my bed.

He takes a few steps forward and leans over to look at the
top sheet. "I'm not really fluent, you know. I just know enough
Rubezi to get by."

I glance up at the camera then meet his eye. My thinking he

can help may be the only thing keeping him alive right now. "Then tell them you need a scientist who speaks a little English to help with the technical stuff."

His chin inclines a barely perceptible amount before he turns to the guards and speaks to them in Rubezi. One pulls a walkie talkie from his belt and relays the message.

Casilla turns back to me. "It's true, then. You caught the virus."

I nod.

He looks back down at the papers, craning his neck to read with his good eye.

"Here, let me at least get you a chair."

The guards jump when I get up, but I hold my hands up in front of me then point to an empty chair near the foot of the bed and they relax again. Scooting it up to the head of the bed, I find myself leaning on it and breathing harder than should be necessary. When Casilla is seated, I lay back down on the bed and close my eyes to steady myself, but when I close them, pressure builds behind my eyes and my head starts to ache. Opening them, Casilla's battered face comes into focus. He's worried.

I force a smile. "I'm fine. So read what you can. I'll tell you when to skip ahead."

The corner of his lip quivers as if he would smile, but the smile never materializes. "You'll have to turn the pages for me."

I nod and turn to lay on my side facing him so I can reach the stand.

He clears his throat. "Notes of Doctor Ekrem Muhadow, Lead Scientist, WHISP research—"

"Skip ahead."

———

"A COMPOUND OF MICROSCOPIC...SOMETHING... ROBOTS?" Casilla points with a recently freed hand at the word giving him trouble.

My brain whirs to life at the thought of nanotechnology. "Like nanites? I thought those weren't possible."

Glasses perched on the end of his nose, the scientist, Vural, squints down at the page then looks up as if the translation hovers in the air just above his head. "Ah, electromagnetic."

Casilla nods, "Oh. That makes more sense. Electromagnetic particles made of..." he points again.

The scientist checks the word. "Platinum."

Casilla sighs. "Platinum." He takes a deep breath and rubs his eye. "Can we pause for a minute?"

I nod. "Of course."

He sips some water.

"So, it was really our government that made WHISPs?" I ask.

Casilla frowns. "It's not as simple as that. We commissioned a technology that allowed for the creation of WHISPs."

"And the people who made the virus tried to steal it back, and tried to kill us?"

"A small splinter group trying to put Pandora back in her box."

I consider correcting his analogy, but don't really have the strength for it. "By killing all the WHISPers? Won't there just be more with time?"

He shakes his head. "I'm thinking they were hoping the virus would persist and kill as new WHISPs were developing. Or maybe they were just planning on releasing more on a regular basis." He takes another sip of water. "Anyway, is any of this"—he points to the stack of notes we're not even halfway through—"making sense? Anything helping?"

I really want to say yes, but I can't. "Not yet, but I know

that platinum is what some cancer drugs are made of and that they fight cancer by zapping it with electricity or something."

The phone on the wall rings with a sound right out of the 1950s. The three of us just stare at it through two solid rings before Casilla makes eye contact with the guards and motions answering it. The tallest guard trains his gun on Casilla and nods. Rolling his eyes, Casilla rises and answers on the fourth ring. "Wanda's House of Pain."

I widen my eyes and Vural's face clouds with confusion.

I turn to him. "It's a joke."

Vural looks unconvinced, but we both turn back to Casilla when he says, "I'll let her know." He hangs up the receiver and faces me. "That was your hubby. He says he thinks the amplifier is almost ready to test."

"Oh. Good."

"Don't sound so happy about it." Casilla returns to his chair.

I lean back into my pillow. "It's just that I'm not really sure I know yet how to tweak it so it won't kill me."

"Ahh, details, details." He picks up the last page he was reading. "Now, where were we?"

———

I'M BOUNCING A BABY ON MY KNEE. SHE COOS AND gurgles and I smile at her while making googly noises. But then I can't hold her. My fingers are going right through her like she's made of water. "No!" The color fades from her cheeks until they are a dull gray, and the color continues to leach away until her eyes are solid, unseeing rain clouds. The gray runs down her arms to her chubby fingers. "Stop it!" Then it spreads down to her legs and plump toes. "Please!" The baby shadow bursts like a balloon then fades away until I'm clutching at smoke.

"Sylvy!"

I jolt awake and hold back a wave of nausea, my fingers grasping at the thin blanket of the hospital bed. Images from the dream cling to my mind like cobwebs. "I lost her."

"Shhh, it's all right, everything's all right." It isn't until Ben's stroking my face that I realize he's here.

The horror of the dream fades only to be replaced by the horror of reality, and my stomach knots again.

"Thought we'd lost you." Casilla emerges from behind Ben.

I try to smile. "Sorry, I must've fallen asleep."

"Can't imagine why. I've only been reading you the most action-packed of these notes."

The notes. I try to remember anything from them that might help tune the amplifier. "Do the notes list a frequency for the virus?"

"Frequency?" Casilla looks a bit mystified.

Ben brushes my hair back, then picks up the stack of papers. "Let me check." He skims three pages before pointing and holding the paper up to Casilla. "What's that number?"

Casilla frowns. "A dosage, I think."

Nodding, Ben skips through a few more pages, then pauses, "Here it is," and hands the paper to Casilla.

"The particles vibrate at a frequency of 11 Hertz, which seems to have a greater effect on the WHISP particles than expected. Over time a..." He holds his thumb under a word and takes the paper to Vural.

Vural squints. "Destructive."

"Destructive...." Casilla points again.

"Ah, loop. No, not loop. Ah, cycle. Yes, cycle." Vural nods.

"Destructive cycle develops."

Ben nods. "That makes sense. Extremely low frequency vibrations can be harmful to the human body, and if they reached a resonant vibration with the WHISP particles—"

"But is that even possible? I thought my WHISP's frequency

was different from Lincoln's. How can it reach resonance to different frequencies?" I'm not sure I even know what I'm talking about.

Ben frowns. "I'm not sure, but certain biological viruses adapt to host conditions to become more virulent. Maybe it's something like that. There is a viral vector involved, isn't there?" He turns to Vural.

Vural nods then frowns. "Yes, but is complicated." He makes a gesture with his hands as if trying to make two parts of a ball fit together.

"Does that really matter?" Casilla shrugs. "If you know the frequency of the virus, can't you just blast it with the opposite frequency? Like cancel it out?"

"It doesn't exactly work like that. You can block sound, certain frequencies, but I don't know how you would do that between the virus and a person's WHISP without blocking the person from their WHISP, and that's"—Ben glances at me —"bad. Also, if the virus is somehow already integrated into the WHISP, you couldn't block it."

Casilla glares at me. "So, how did you cure it before?"

I thought happy thoughts. I clear my throat. Even in my head, the answer sounds stupid. Breaking away from Casilla's gaze, I look to Ben. "Is there a, um, happiness frequency?"

"A happiness frequency?" Casilla snorts.

Ben's forehead wrinkles like a theatre curtain rising. "No. It's a real thing, musical healing and special frequencies encouraging DNA repair. They use it in Alzheimer patients sometimes."

My shoulders sag with relief. *I'm not crazy. Well, at least not about this.* "But it was more than that, I think. I also used Liv somehow."

"Maybe she acted as the vector...." By his unfocused eyes, I know Ben is talking mostly to himself.

"So, we need a WHISP?"
Casilla's words weigh down my heart.
We need a WHISP.

CHAPTER 37

Operation Shade: Debriefing [name redacted] – 04015
Audio Transcription Excerpt
Agent: Would you classify the mission as a success?
[name redacted]: Depends on what you mean by
success.

MY EYES FIND CASILLA'S. "No."

"But who else can we explain this to?"

"Not an option."

His eyes turn hard as diamonds. "Don't think you're the only one I'm trying to save here. If we can't cure his people, do you think the president is letting any of us out of here alive?"

"What? What's he talking about, Sylvy?" Ben's back with us again.

"He wants to use Lincoln."

Ben doesn't say anything.

No. "Ben, he wants to expose our son to a deadly virus."

Ben opens his mouth, but then closes it again.

"Hasn't he already been exposed?" Casilla lifts his open hands.

I'm back in the WHISP cellblock in Yedys watching the ex-

CIA thug open the virus vial and feeling the droplets hit my face as he flings the contents into the air. Lincoln was exposed, and he's okay, but it doesn't mean he wasn't just lucky. "We don't know that he's immune."

"I'm calling him." Casilla turns.

I'm up and on top of Casilla before I can even think, my arms closing around his thick throat. Then everything goes dark and I'm back on the bed, unsure if I only imagined attacking him.

Gasping, crimson-faced, eyes burning, Casilla glares at me.

I guess I did.

Ben takes my good hand in his and squeezes it. I want to squeeze back, but my hand's gone numb. "Sylvy, I know you want to protect Lincoln"—his voice chokes off and he swallows hard—"but I think we're running out of time."

Betrayal stabs through me like a white-hot poker. "We don't even know if he can do this with Leo." The words taste bitter.

"He said he used Leo to set off the sprinklers in the cellblock."

He's right, Lincoln used Leo in the cellblock and to fight the rogue CIA agent's WHISP, and I'm almost certain Lincoln also used Leo to short circuit the president's WHISP suppressor, but I turn away. I can't consent to risking Lincoln's life. I can't. Not after everything we went through to get him back. I'm mad at myself for saying anything about using Liv. *Liv*. I turn back to Ben. "Let me try it with Liv first."

Ben hesitates. "You said she wasn't responding."

"I was afraid to try too hard without...before we had a plan. Now we have a plan. And the happy frequency will probably help." *Maybe*.

A skeptical frown pulls at Ben's mouth. "Syvly, I—"

"Please, Ben. Can we please just try?"

"But I could lose you both." His voice is like a broken toy

and I'm not sure if he means me and the baby or me and Lincoln.

With effort, I manage to squeeze his hand. "I can do this." *I think I can. I hope we can.*

Ben nods. "All right, but I want Casilla to go get Lincoln and have him ready just in case."

I only nod because I know he won't agree otherwise. "Okay."

Ben turns to Casilla. "Go."

He flashes me a dark look before turning to the nearest guard and speaking in Rubezi. After rolling his eyes, the guard recuffs Casilla's wrists behind his back and the two of them plus a second guard exit the room.

Ben kisses my forehead then turns to what looks like a pile of random electronics on a cart. Upon further inspection, I recognize a few of the bits from the amplifier and some parts that look like other WHISP equipment Ben's used on me in the past.

"Do you remember the happy frequency?"

He doesn't look at me but continues to adjust cords and dials. "Not exactly."

Oh shit.

"Try 741 Hertz."

We both stare at Vural.

"Mother has cancer. Listens to healing music after her treatments. It has helped. Also 432 and 538."

I look to Ben. He nods and adjusts more dials then pulls out what looks like two suction cups attached to wires. He comes to the side of the bed with them. "This isn't how I wanted to do it, but I have to stick these to your temples."

"Okay."

As he wets them with gel from a tube and secures them to my head, I can't help but think of old sci-fi movies about reanimating corpses, mind control, and frying people's brains. I swallow hard.

He meets my eyes. "You doing okay?"

I nod, not trusting my voice.

He looks like he's about to say more, but then kisses me so gently it's like a butterfly's wing brushing my lips. I close my eyes, but then the air shifts, and when I open them, he's back at the cart flipping switches. A soft hum fills the air and one of the guards still in the room flinches and fingers his gun. Maybe he thought the device was some kind of bomb.

"Get ready, Sylvy, I'm going to turn it on."

I nod and close my eyes again.

"Three, two—"

I reach out to Liv and meet the wall of tar again. This time I press my hands into it, pushing, stretching, and trying to make a hole, struggling to get to Liv. But as the blackness gives way, my hands get stuck inside of it. I try to yank them back, but the tar has turned to millions of shapeless, crawling insects and they're skittering up my arms. I want to scream but the thought of letting the things into my mouth keeps my lips pressed together. Within the churning movement of the creatures, the vibration pulses against my skin like the suckling of an oily, toothless mouth. Tentative at first, it's growing stronger. Pain grips my chest as my heart races. I try to push the oozing swarm back with my foot, but only succeed in allowing the flowing pitch to climb up my leg. A part of my brain is screaming at me to think happy thoughts, but I can't think about anything other than the pulsating ichor slowly engulfing me.

A sound like a distant bell echoes around me, and the vibration changes. Not a lot, but enough to slow the progression of the living, black slime. Enough that I'm able to shake my leg free and dig in my heels to get leverage to free my arms. *It's working! Ben, it's working!* I think the words as loud as I can, wondering what my body looks like right now. *Am I thrashing in the bed or am I just lying there still? Can he hear me?* One of my arms pulls free and I chance calling out, "Liv! Liv, I'm here. We have to fight it! Where are you?"

Something is tugging at my ankles. At first, I think it might be Liv, but when I look down, tendrils of darkness are snaking around both legs as an obsidian pool forms under my feet. The low, unclean vibration radiates up through my soles, sneaking through gaps in the new vibration. Like a minor note in a major key, it sours the melody. Trying to remember the music, I start humming, but it's too late. It's all been drowned out by the discordant harmony of the vibration. My calves tickle as innumerable legs find my ankles and then my knees. I brush frantically at my legs with my free hand, but it comes away coated and itching. "No! Stop!"

Music like the song of a wind chime cuts through the cacophony. It's as clear as a mountain stream and I can almost see through the wall of virus as the waves of the vibration are flung apart by each tone. The dark pool under me recedes and the black globs on my fingers drip away. My other hand slides easily from inside the tar wall which is now still dark but shimmering like water. I take a deep breath to steady myself and concentrate. *Seeing Lincoln alive in the lab. The warmth of Ben's arms around me when I thought he was dead. Finding the hole in the wall when I couldn't climb out of the prison camp.* Buoyed by the calming chimes, I wrap happy thoughts around me like armor and prepare to plunge through the barrier.

I take a step forward but stop short. *Finding out I'm pregnant at fifty-four.* I stare at the shimmering surface in front of me. *What if it hurts the baby? What if we cure all the prisoners and the president and he still executes us all? Or what if we cure them and he imprisons us here and forces us to research a WHISP cure? What if all this, all we went through, is for nothing?* I find myself on my knees, the watery tar trickling toward me like living mercury.

No. None of that matters right now. The only reason we're all alive is because the president thinks that he's been exposed to the virus, which is true, and that I can cure him. *If I can't cure myself, if I die, if he thinks I lied to him, what will he do to Ben and Lincoln?* And if I don't survive, there's no chance for the baby. I get up on one knee then heave myself up to standing. *You can do this, Sylvy. You're strong. You've done it before.*

I throw back my shoulders and plunge headlong into...darkness.

CHAPTER 38

Recovered File CAW Server
Date: August 12, 2027
WHISP Penetration Test 119: Magnet
The subject's WHISP was positioned between two 6 feet
by 3 feet magnetic sheets. The subject reported no ill
effects upon initial positioning. Gradually, the space
between the sheets was shortened at 2-centimeter inter-
vals. The subject reported only mild discomfort in the
form of a headache. The seizure did not occur until the
sheets were only 4 centimeters apart and fully immersed
in the subject's WHISP.

I MAY HAVE MADE A MISTAKE.

I can't breathe. I'm drowning in deep waters. Dragging my
arms and legs through the liquid, I can't tell which direction
the surface is, or if there even is a surface. Any positive
thoughts have abandoned me and sunk into the abyss around
me. Now I'm sinking, too, the weight of the water crushing
down on my chest. I stop moving and let the darkness embrace
me. In the stillness, something brushes against my eardrums.

It's a bubble bobbing to the surface and, in that moment, I remember the sound of wind chimes. *Lincoln. Ben. Baby.*

Fight, dammit!

Then I'm thrashing upward, kicking and screaming silent screams from a throat with no air. But now the surface is clear. An arc of light with a figure outlined against the brilliance. *Liv? Help me.* A gray hand reaches down into the water and my fingertips brush past. Just a little farther. But the bare space between my hand and my savior's is a chasm and my strength is waning. I thought I could do this alone, but I need help.

"Mom?"

The hand grips my wrist and pulls.

I suck sweet air into my lungs so sharply I cough. *I'm alive! I think.* I open my eyes, see Lincoln, and stop breathing again. *No. He shouldn't be exposed.* I try to tell him to get away from me, but I choke on the words.

"It's okay. I think it's okay." Lincoln meets my eyes. "How do you feel?"

"I...you shouldn't...." I raise a hand in a feeble attempt to push him away.

"Be saving your life?" Ben steps forward.

"What?"

"I know I promised to let you try to cure the virus without him, but you were unconscious and it didn't seem like the first frequency was working, so I had to bring in Lincoln. He and Leo, well...." Ben looks at Lincoln.

"I think we stopped it. I can't feel it around you anymore, but I want to be sure. Do you feel up to reaching out to Liv?"

Anger, relief, fear, and a soup of other emotions are roiling in my stomach. I want to hug and smack Ben in equal measures, and hug and scream at Lincoln all at once. Instead, I nod dumbly, take a deep breath, and close my eyes. At first, the fear freezes me with thoughts of getting caught in the crawling tar or drowning in the black void again, but gradually I calm down and reach out.

Where have you been?

I let out the breath I've been holding. *We're okay.* The discordant vibration is gone.

I open my eyes and can't hide the relief on my face. Ben's shoulders slide down as the tension leaves them and Lincoln's mouth breaks into a wide grin. My urge to leap out of the bed into Ben's arms almost overwhelms me, but suddenly I feel as if I haven't slept in months.

"I might need—"

The door bursts open and guards flood into the small room. The fact that we're still prisoners in Rubezikan is abruptly knife-blade sharp. Out of fight, I can only sigh. A guard with a feather in his hat steps forward.

"The president summons you."

Of course, he does.

———

TURNS OUT PRESIDENT PARGULMAHAMADOMET himself wasn't infected by the virus. It's not a surprise, since he didn't come anywhere near Lincoln or me. About half the WHISPers still alive in the cellblock had been infected, but with Lincoln's and my help and Ben's machine, we cured all but two who were near death for other reasons I couldn't let myself wonder too much about. Then, a bunch of fast talking from Casilla, the backing of Lincoln's contacts among the scientists, and the promise of large sums of money and non-interference from the U.S. government won us an official presidential pardon.

Back in a truck trundling across the stifling Rubezikan desert, each bump in the non-existent road instigating a new bruise on my ass, I can't help but smile.

Casilla catches my expression. "What're you so happy about?"

I gesture to the cramped, sweltering space around us. "This. We're out of that god-forsaken, marble hell. We didn't die. I found my son. We're going home."

He snorts. "*You* found your son?"

I roll my eyes. "Fine. We found my son...." A smile dies before it reaches my lips. That wasn't Casilla's mission, at all.

"What?"

"Nothing."

He raises an eyebrow.

I frown. "It's just...that was never even your mission."

The question on his face is replaced by a scowl. "No, not the—"

"Primary mission, I know, I know." But my mind keeps spinning. "Your primary mission was to lure the rogue CIA agents into a trap."

"You can understand why I couldn't tell you that."

"Yeah, but...."

Casilla adjusts his position on the bench as the truck grinds over a particularly large rock. "But what?"

"If it was a trap, why'd we almost get blown up and the bad guys almost got away with the virus?"

His frown darkens. "Because our communications got cut." He shoots a quick glance at Ben out of the corner of his eye.

Ben's conversation with a more-or-less-jovial Manganaro stutters to a stop as, sensing the sparks of an argument, they both look our way.

Anger bubbles in the back of my throat, tasting of bile. "And why was Ben in charge of the most important thing in the whole mission anyway? If you were trying to draw them into a trap, you should've known that communications would be the weak point."

"Hey, your husband lived; we had a contingency plan."

"Blowing up all our communications is one hell of a contingency plan. You should've known they'd go after the communications. You should've had someone there with experience. Someone who knew there'd be agents coming, who'd be ready for them and could take them out without having to blow the whole truck."

Something shifts behind Casilla's eyes. "He was less of a risk there."

"Less of a risk by himself? Less of a risk with the success of the whole mission riding on him?"

"Just what the hell are you saying, Harbinger?"

Manganaro's voice is cold even in the hot truck, "She's saying you're a traitor, boss."

I glance at Manganaro. His gun is out and aimed at Casilla's gut. The only sound now is the rev of the truck's engine and thunk of debris against the undercarriage. Valcross, Jones, and Lincoln have stopped their impromptu blackjack game, and one of the cards slips off the bench onto the floor of the truck as the silence stretches.

Casilla looks from me to Manganaro, to Ben, to the rest of the group, then back to Manganaro. "This is crazy. I didn't even want him there."

Cold sweat trickles down the back of my neck as I reach for Casilla's gun. "Oh really? Because I'm pretty sure you were the one who convinced me he'd fuck up the mission if he came with us." I slide the gun out of his holster and level it at him.

Casilla's eyes go wider. "It wasn't supposed to be him in the truck."

"Who was it supposed to be then?" It's hard to get the words through my clenched teeth.

A strangled cry from my left distracts me. My eyes dart to Lincoln. Valcross has an arm wrapped around his throat and a gun at his temple.

"Me." Valcross's face is blank. "It vas supposed to be me."

CHAPTER 39

Department of Homeland Security Internal Communication
Hana Siddiqui
Re: New York WHISP Task Force
Despite the assurances of a Detective Crone, a very new addition to the WHISP Task Force, that temporary Chief Sylvia Harbinger is in Washington being "debriefed," I cannot locate a single person who knows which federal department is administering this so-called debriefing nor can I find a registered guest of any hotel in the greater DC area going by her name.

ALL I CAN THINK AS I TURN MY GUN ON VALCROSS IS: not Valcross. I like Valcross. Casilla I could see as a cynical traitor. But not Valcross.

"Did you know I was turned down for Wonder Soldier Program? Something about my DNA not being right. Is bullshit. And then everybody and mother gets to have powers? No. I think not."

Casilla turns casually to Manganaro. "Shoot him."

"You got it, boss."

Valcross shakes the hand of the arm around Lincoln's neck. "Ah, ahh. I wouldn't do it. Unless you want we should all explode." In that hand is a grenade sans pin. He turns his gaze on me. "And don't you think funny WHISP business or I blow son's brains out before we all go boom." He glances around the back of the truck at everyone's stunned faces. "Good. Now put down guns."

I have to force myself to drop Casilla's gun when every instinct in me is screaming not to. But I can't find another choice. Manganaro and Jones likewise place their guns on the floor of the truck.

"Now, Benjamin. You collect guns and drop out back of truck."

Ben's face is made of stone, but he does as he's told and then sits back down between Manganaro and Casilla. While Valcross is watching Ben, Casilla catches my eye. He knows. I dropped his gun, but not my own. The CIA agents, acting as soldiers, all carry theirs in holsters outside their fatigues, but I'm a cop. I only feel comfortable when my holster is tucked inside my jacket. Now, I have to figure out how to use it without getting us all killed.

"Casilla. You will tell driver there's been change of plan. We go back to Bez Imeni."

Comprehension dawning, I blink. "The explosion. The firefight."

"Dah. I thought why do this thing at Yedys with all going well? If some should die early"—he shrugs—"is less to deal with later."

Jones shakes his head. "You right bastard."

When Valcross turns his attention to Jones, Casilla closes the gap between us on the bench and reaches his hand up under my shirt to my gun, but he's not quite quick enough. As he pulls it out and aims at Valcross, Valcross turns and tutts at him.

"Do you really think to be fast enough to shoot me then catch grenade?"

Casilla gives me a sidelong glance. "Not me."

I realize what he wants me to do a second before he shoots. Liv and I lunge forward, grab the grenade, and shove Valcross's pistol away from Lincoln's head. Shots ring out but I can't concentrate on anything but squeezing the grenade's handle with Liv's insubstantial fingers.

"Harbinger!"

I open my eyes, but then gasp and try to connect with Liv again, waiting for the flash. But someone's shaking me.

"Harbinger, it's okay. Jones put a pin in it."

I open my eyes again. It's Casilla. I turn my head and find Valcross dead on the floor of the truck and Ben clumsily hugging Lincoln as we continue to bump roughly along. Ben gives me a weak smile, and I break free of Casilla to hug them both before collapsing on the floor next to Lincoln. I sniff and find tears in my eyes.

"Jesus, Harbinger, I thought you were going to shoot me." Casilla offers me my gun, handle first.

I bark a small, near-hysterical laugh. "I almost did." I glance over at Valcross's body. "Why did he confess? Why not just let me shoot you?"

"Because I was about to tell you that he was supposed to stay in the truck and handle communications, or maybe he thought he had the upper hand with that grenade, or maybe he thought something would give him away at the inquest." He lifts his shoulders in a half-shrug. "Or maybe he was just an idiot."

Lincoln looks at me a little awestruck. "How did you know there was a traitor, Mom?"

I put on my best "duh" face. "I'm actually a pretty decent detective when I'm not out masquerading as a CIA agent."

"About that." Casilla rubs his chin. "The agency would be

lucky to have you. I could put in a good word. You know, on account of you saving my life and all."

My eyebrows find my disheveled hairline. "Just one small problem with that. Did you forget that I'm pregnant?"

He looks pointedly at my stomach. "You'd be surprised how well that works to get people to let their guard down."

I start to laugh, but then I'm not sure he's joking, and the idea that he isn't sickens me. Trying to shake off my disgust, I shrug. "That's okay. I spent enough of my firstborn's childhood away on cases. Maybe I will actually retire this time."

Ben squeezes my shoulder and I lean my head back against his leg.

I take Lincoln's hand in my good hand. "Now, can we please get on a plane that will take me and my family back home?"

Casilla clears his throat. "About that."

———

CRONE SETS DOWN A FILE HE'S BEEN PERUSING AS I approach his desk. "Nice of you to join us."

I gesture around the department. "What, no balloons, no cake?"

He grunts. "Maybe if you were sticking around for a while. From what I hear, you're only here to clean out your desk."

I pat my now slightly egregious belly. "Nope. Maternity leave doesn't start for another two weeks, believe it or not."

"That so?"

I glance around. "I see Homeland Security's cleared out."

"It's been almost seven months."

I lower myself into a chair. "Really? That long?"

He shakes his head. "Harbinger."

"Yeah."

"Are you really going to make me ask where you've been for

seven months or why you were allowed back on the freakin' job like nothing happened?"

I lean forward conspiratorially. "I could tell you."

Crone leans in.

"But then I'd have to kill you."

"Oh, fuck you, Harbinger. I thought we were partners. I even joined this goddamn task force for you."

My smile is bitter. "No, seriously. It's classified. You wouldn't believe the bullshit they had me sign." I lean back. "Also, I kinda don't feel like reliving it."

Crone sighs. "I guess that's fair. You do look like ten miles of shit." He leans back, too. "But seriously, you coming back after this kiddo comes or what?"

"Haven't gotten that far yet, but how many chiefs do you know with kids?"

"Didn't the chief have two daughters?"

The corners of my mouth tug down. "Yeah, he did. I mean babies."

"First time for everything. Also, technically, the head of the task force isn't a chief."

I snort a sharp chuckle. "What? You really missed me that much?"

He shrugs. "Maybe."

I heave myself back up to my feet. "I'll think about it."

"That's all I ask."